In Which Brief Stories Are Told

Phillip Sterling

In Which
Brief

Stories
Are Told

Wayne State University Press Detroit

15 14 13 12 11   5 4 3 2 1

Library of Congress Cataloging-in-Publication Data

Sterling, Phillip.
In which brief stories are told / Phillip Sterling.
p. cm. — (Made in Michigan writers series)
ISBN 978-0-8143-3507-9 (pbk. : alk. paper)
I. Title.
PS3569.T38795I5 2011
813'.54—dc22
2010031652

Designed and typeset by Maya Rhodes
Composed in Leitura

To Jane

For, while the tale of how we suffer, and how we are delighted, and how we may triumph is never new, it always must be heard.

—James Baldwin, "*Sonny's Blues*"

Contents

One Version of the Story

The first time Richardson comes in, me and Bruce are backed against a red S-15, having coffee and shooting the breeze about the Cowboy-Steelers game. We're just hanging there, gabbing, when this buckskin '76 Century Custom wheels in at a good clip, swings around, and lurches to a stop, smack in front of the double doors, as if it was meant for the showroom—if the Jimmy we were leaning on wasn't in its place. A blast of frigid air seems to shoulder the guy in the door.

Right away I'm struck by what he's wearing—or what he's not, actually—no overcoat or nothing, just a plain brownish-gray suit, and it's only about twenty outside. Still, he's dressed pretty snazzy, with the right kind of tie, and I decide at the get-go that he could turn out to be a good mark. Fact is, he's coming hard, like he knows what he's in for. That's usually a good sign.

Of course, Bruce catches the scent same as I do. I see him roll his eyes—he means for me to see—like we both know the guy's only going to be a bother and Bruce is sorry our little chat's interrupted. But I know better. When it comes to sales, Bruce is a carnivore. He begins to sidle toward the guy right off, even while he's still blabbing to me about the game, because January's been slower than usual, and old Bruce is a pressure point, always sizing up prospects with one side of his brain as he figures commission with the other. I'm sure he was pushing to get a jump on Sales Master of the Model Year, since I've beaten him out the last two seasons. But just as Bruce moves full stride toward the guy, waving off my smart-aleck comeback, Lucy pages him for an urgent on line two, and I get to belly up for the sale.

That's when I first notice the guy's a little anxious. He never really stands still the whole time we talk. He's maybe five-ten or eleven and a little paunchy in the gut. I guessed mid-thirties, with some gray hair just beginning to show at the temples, like owl tufts. His suit coat's unbuttoned, and his white shirt pulls kind of wrinkly at the waistband of his pants, just about where his bluish-tinted tie points.

All of a sudden, I'm beginning to have doubts about my prospects, like maybe I overestimated him. Fact is, he's looking sort of lackey—like he doesn't want our eyes to meet. He stares out the window as we talk.

Still, I'm thinking *upgrade*, maybe a Regal. But before I can even slip him one of my cards or pop a wintergreen Certs in my mouth, he's asking if we have anything with four doors, says he's looking for something with four doors.

"Well, you have quite a choice," I begin, lifting my voice to that friendly twang I was told helps sway the just-lookings into sixty-month payments. I sweep the air with my arm, figuring to bat his gaze out the west window and into the front lot, where dozens of our fastest movers gleam like enamel candy. But I no sooner start to list our latest models and options when he cuts me short.

"Four doors," he says. "It's for my wife."

I'm thinking: *Hot damn.* I can't believe my luck. Seems like I had him pegged right all along. It just so happened we *did* have something with four doors, a unit we'd taken in on a dealer trade—from Indiana, I think. It was a white Cutlass sedan with aquamarine interior—pretty dull, actually—and Bruce and me had a hefty side bet going as to who could unload it first. I mean, activity on that unit was like zero—so bad that Danny, our service manager, had been using it as a short-term loaner. Except for the one hick whose sheepdog upchucked on the back seat, it hadn't gotten much use, maybe two thousand on the odometer.

I figure I can still pass it off as a demonstrator, so I begin to describe it to the guy—"Walt Richardson," he says his name is. But again he stops me. Again he asks me if it has four doors. Again I tell him it does. Next thing I know, he reaches into his suit coat and pulls out from his breast pocket one of those checkbook-sized wallets serious players like to carry. I can see that it's fat with bills—hundreds, maybe larger—like he'd just stopped at NBD and gotten them. He says that if the price is right, he'll pay cash.

About then I begin to wonder if the Cutlass was still parked outside the service door, like the last time I'd seen it, or if it had been loaned out, or if it was even cleaned up enough for us to take it for a test drive. So I tell Richardson that if he can wait I'd have it brung around, though it'd be a matter of some minutes, since I'd have to hang dealer tags and such—figuring the guys could maybe clean it up a little on the way. He says, "Just give me your best price."

I admit, I had trouble believing it myself. I'd been hustling cars for twenty-three years by then—the first seven with American Motors, the rest with GM. I don't recall many easy sales early in the season. Mostly January's slow—lookers with too little Christmas money. Probably why I remember this one so well. When I ask him about a trade, he nods toward the Buick. So I help him to a cup of coffee—two creams—settle him in my cubicle, and slip on my parka. Then me and Bob, our Sales Manager, go out to appraise his car.

Like I said, I couldn't believe my luck. The Century was in

good condition, with many of the more popular options—auto and air, power sunroof, a V-6. And it was clean. Fact is, it looked like Richardson had just come back from a car wash, though I don't know of any that might have been open in that weather. Even so, the mud flaps dripped icicles of what looked like soapy water. Except for a screwed up headlight and some slight damage to the right front bumper, like from an indirect hit on a garage door or a deer, the car had good resale value.

We took a chance, since Richardson acted kind of eager, and underbid the book price of the Buick a good grand—given the damage. Then I knocked off two percent from the Cutlass sticker. I figured it would be a place to start, and we could bargain to terms. But Richardson surprised me. He said he'd take it.

Okay, I may have been a little suspicious then. I mean, the guy didn't even flinch when I said it was a demonstrator. He said again that it didn't really matter—as long as it had four doors—it was going to be his wife's car. Well, if it didn't matter to him, it surely didn't matter to me. I was about to make a good week's commission on the sale—and so soon after Christmas. I didn't press him for *why*. I just sold him the car.

Out of habit, I dallied a few minutes in Bob's office—listening to him brag about his cruise to the Caribbean over the holidays—while he initialed the offer. When I get back to my cubicle and congratulate Richardson on the deal, he thumbs open the wallet and starts dealing bills on my blotter. Next thing I know, Bruce saunters in with a set of keys for me—not that I need them, of course; it's just so he can nosey up on how the deal's going. I admit, I was feeling pretty good by then. So I ask Bruce to see if service can prep the Cutlass right away. Well, Bruce's face turns sort of metallic and his eyes bug out. He knows it's going to cost him. Thinking then that I might be able to salt Bruce's wound, I mention undercoating to Richardson, and, sure enough, he just flips out a couple more hundreds to the pile. Bruce about keels over.

Within an hour, Richardson was on his way home in a white Cutlass Supreme.

We ended up unloading the buckskin-colored Buick at auction. We'd made such a good trade that it wasn't worth our effort to fix it up enough to put it on the lot. It was in great shape for an auction bid, though, and we did well on it.

After that, Richardson became a regular. Every couple years or so, he'd come and trade what he had for something new. Of course, he wised up some over the years—each time I had to work him a little harder—but it was never *real* work; each time I knew he'd be an easy sway. Even with his wife there. Except for that first time, when he'd brought in the Century, his wife came along with him, and she always drove. *Mary*, I think, or some other common name. A small, quiet woman. Had she come in by herself, I would have guessed her to be the unmarried type. She never interfered much in our deals, never appeared to care, in spite of Richardson's repeated insistence: "It's for my wife." What sparked the marriage is beyond me. Waiting with them in my office for paperwork, I imagined countless hours of dull glances cast about their family room, a routine so engaging as to be numb.

At Christmas each year, Richardson would send me a card thanking me for the calendar our office sent out to him.

Then, about three years ago, six months after I sold them a silver Calais, he came in alone. He said he was sorry, but he needed to return the car, if it was still possible. If we couldn't buy the Calais back, he said, he would understand, but then he wondered if I knew anyone that would be willing to accept it as a gift. At first, I thought he was pulling my leg. He'd never appeared to have been unhappy before. I assumed it had something to do with his wife, since she wasn't with him. Perhaps she'd decided that she could no longer look disappointment in the eye. Still, I assured him that we could fix whatever the problem was.

He sort of laughed. He said there was nothing wrong with

the vehicle. He just didn't need it anymore. It was his wife's car, after all, and now that she had left him, he didn't want it. He didn't want anything to do with it. In fact, he said, bringing the car over was the first time he had driven in years, and he wasn't about to drive it back. He no longer had a license. He would call a taxi to take him home.

Obviously, I had to check with Bob on that one. We didn't have a buy-back policy ourselves, though at the time the Ford dealers may have been advertising one. Bob considered that, I think, when he gave me the go-ahead—since Richardson was a regular—if he'd negotiate on the first year's depreciation and if there was nothing wrong with the car. We went out together to see. Another surprise! The Calais still had the paper floor mats we'd put in six months before, and the odometer barely registered three hundred miles. To top it off, when we offered ten percent under depreciation, Richardson said "Fine."

I should have known then, of course. I should have recognized the warning. "Fine" is not something a car salesman often hears. Like "easy," it's a word that rarely exists in our profession.

It was shortly after that, as we were waiting for the paperwork to clear, that Richardson began to tell me all about his New Year's celebration eleven years before. He said he needed to tell me because he didn't think we'd ever see each other again and because it had been bothering him for a long time. Because I'd been so nice to him, so helpful. He said he thought I'd understand.

He couldn't remember driving home that New Year's Eve. They'd been to a party—friends of his wife. At first he'd felt uncomfortable; such events usually didn't sit well with him. However, it being New Year's and all, he'd warmed to the occasion with a few drinks. Quite a few. So many, in fact, that he hadn't wanted to leave when his wife insisted they go, and he'd stayed at the party long after she'd gotten a ride home.

He assumed that he had driven himself back to their house.

But he couldn't remember. And that's why it bothered him so much when, on the day after New Year's, he saw the damage to the right front bumper of that buckskin tan Century Custom.

He was on his way to work, he said, walking around the front of the car to open the garage door, when he first noticed the broken headlight and a slight dent in the hood. When he looked closer, he saw what appeared to be dried blood on the grille and a scrap of fuzzy material, like from a winter coat—he was convinced that it was clothing—caught in the plastic trim near the fender wall. Could he have been in an accident and not remember? he asked.

Before I could answer, he said, "Apparently so." He had panicked then, cleaned up the car as best he could, and he'd never told his wife. A week later he'd traded it for the white Cutlass.

As he told his story, I began to feel cold, like when Bob turns on the air conditioning too early in the spring. I first wondered if it was the coffee—I'd been drinking more than usual that week—or if was because I hadn't had enough for breakfast. But then I realized it wasn't in my stomach. It seemed to be coming from a place in my body that I didn't know was there. A feeling I'd never felt before. A feeling of disbelief, perhaps. Or uncertainty. Richardson had always impressed me as being reserved, too wimpy a kind of guy to have been blind drunk—that out of control—even on New Year's Eve. He'd always impressed me as kind of shy, maybe even pussy-whipped.

On the other hand, when I thought about it, before that moment he'd never really shared very much about his personal life. Maybe I just didn't know any better. It was about then I noticed how much he'd aged since that January day when he'd first pulled up to the double doors. He looked sickly, thin and undernourished. What little hair he had left was nearly white; he appeared fifteen years older than what he probably was. I recalled how odd he had acted at our initial meeting. And it was also just about then that I glanced at my reflection in the small mirror near the door and for the first time, perhaps, didn't want to face the person I saw.

I started to ask him if he'd ever found out for sure if there'd been an accident—but he interrupted my question with a wave of his hand. He told me that for days he had searched through the newspaper and watched TV for information; there hadn't been any. He had called the hospitals for word of unexplained deaths or injuries. There were none. He even gave himself up to the police—admitted to a hit-and-run—but they had no record of any. He said he began to wonder if he had actually hit anything or not. The car *had* been damaged, hadn't it?

When his lengthy pause begged an answer, I said it *had*, if I remembered correctly.

He'd stopped drinking after that. And within the next couple years, he gave up driving. When he drove, he couldn't keep his mind on it. Every animal carcass on the shoulder of the road brought a bad taste to his mouth; every child waiting for a school bus grinned at him like a cartoon skeleton. He began to have trouble keeping to his job, so he lost it. He began to have trouble at every job he tried. He sought therapy, even hypnosis, but nothing helped. He had such terrible dreams that he wouldn't go to sleep for days; then, exhausted, he'd sleep for days without dreaming. And now, finally, his wife, fed up with it all, had left him. It was over. And he couldn't blame her.

You can imagine how uncomfortable I'd grown with Richardson by then, even though his story did kind of explain why he had acted so strange that first day and why the cars were always his wife's and why she had come with him each time. But what I couldn't understand was why he was telling it all to *me*. It had nothing to do with me. It was not my problem. Still, I began to feel a little weird, a little nervous, sort of out of sync with the rest of the world. Like I was beginning to lose a certain advantage, a bit of control. I began to fear that Richardson was more deliberate than he appeared—that he was hatching some foul plot that included me—and that it had something to do with selling him that white Cutlass, a car I had deliberately misrepresented. I tried not to think about it. After all, wasn't that my job? My livelihood?

I wanted him gone. As soon as possible. As far away as possible. I got on the horn to Lucy and begged her to hurry the paperwork. We took back the silver Calais that very afternoon.

That's the last time I saw Walt Richardson, though I think of him occasionally. I mean, imagine living with the guilt of covering up a crime that may never have taken place. Or imagine living all your life in the fear of having done something that you know you'd regret your whole life without ever knowing for sure that you did it. The thought scares me. I've even lost sleep over it. And while I'd like to blame Richardson for that—or the story itself, even though I know it's not mine—placing blame doesn't help. I can't seem to shake it off; it's a burr on my occupation.

There are times when I am driving past children playing by the road and I begin to feel dizzy, so dizzy that I know I should pull over—and yet, I'm afraid that if I do, I will run into something that I'm not seeing. And there are those times I'm just about to close a deal when I break out in a cold sweat. I feel like an accomplice to a crime. That's when I have to excuse myself, to get some fresh air, to put some distance between me and the cheesy smells of new leather and car freshener. For a moment, at least, I need to get away from it, the commission I don't rightly deserve.

Déjà Vu

Years after his father died at MeadowView Nursing Home, where the elder Parker was housed after Alzheimer's turned his memory to a kind of store-brand tartar sauce, Robbie Parker Jr. could not navigate a shopping cart down the seafood aisle of a grocery store without thinking of the night his father had taken him smelting on Crystal Lake.

He'd been roused from a dreamless sleep, snugged into snowsuit and boots, then driven to the boat launch and out onto the ice, to a shanty that, despite its pink color in daylight, darkened the papery surface of the lake like a stubby black crayon.

He'd never been out so late before. Nor would he ever again fill a cooler with so many fish in such little time. During the run, he'd been so busy resetting the hooks on his line that he'd not had time for the thin, bitter cocoa his father had brought in the Thermos, nor the popcorn his mother had sent in a butter-stained grocery sack.

Afterward, the spirits of their breathing paused above the taillights as his father stowed the auger and buckets in the trunk. Robbie shivered. The moonlight was unreal, like night scenes in *Lassie* episodes on their black and white TV, shadows as pronounced as the silhouettes he'd made at Vacation Bible School one Father's Day. The car, however, was warm and close, heady with the smells of fish, kerosene, and cigars. The smells of *men*, thought Robbie.

On the way home, he could barely keep his eyes open. He blew a peephole through the frost on the Mercury's passenger window and calculated how soon he'd cuddle with the green, satin-edged blankie that waited in the warmth of his bed . . .

"Did you have fun?" his father asked suddenly.

"Yessir," Robbie said.

It was remarkable that his father was able to drive at all. While the moon assured for the world at large a visibility as faithful as that of the nightlight in his small bedroom, Robbie could barely make out the road. Snow swirled in the headlights.

"Someday, Robbie," his father said, "I'll be a burden on you. You'll have to take care of me—feed me, bathe me, even change my messy pants . . . Do you know what a *burden* is, Robbie?"

"Yessir," he answered. He was very sleepy.

"Good," said his father. "That's when I hope you remember tonight."

He could recall his mother in her soft nightgown tucking him under his cowboy bedspread, and how he drifted off to the sounds of his parents whispering and laughing as they thumbed the gluey roe from handful after handful of small silver fish.

But it was years later, as he priced seafood in the freezer section at Kroger's, that Robbie knew it would happen, exactly as his father had said.

What We Don't Know

The truck must have pulled in about a quarter to three. I say *about* because I didn't notice exactly. I was flipping through the latest *Cosmo*, delivered the day before, my day off, and I was tickled as usual why so many women would fess up to their foolishness—even make light of it! It never ceases to amaze me how shallow and sex-driven some women actually are, and so I look forward to every month's issue, which I can read during downtime on my shift. I wasn't paying attention to anyone pulling up for gas.

Most purchases that time of night are made at the pump. Have to be. Unless the person wants to prepay at the night window. Store policy requires us to lock the doors between midnight and about five or so, during the hours we're supposed to be mopping and stocking and making coffee—for our own protection, management claims—though I suspect it's more a liability issue, given the tendency to understaff the place, so that most of the night—we're open for gas 24-7—there's just one employee. In my case, that employee is *female*, and so the potential always exists, management thinks, that I could be taken advantage of, robbed or raped or left duct-taped and lifeless in the beer cooler, slumped beside cases of Coronas. Yet more than once I've told Harold—the assistant manager—*Look at me. Does this look like a person you'd want to mess with?* I'm no pathetic little prom queen. I'm five-ten and big boned, as they say. The only girl on the wrestling team in high school, thanks to seasons of haying with my three brothers. For the two years I was at the police academy, few of the male cadets proved to be stronger.

What I mean when I dispute Harold, of course, is *Does this look like a person you'd want to fuck?* I'm not the most attractive, you see, what with the sag of my cheek on the right side, the tuck of scar at the hairline, an eyelid that doesn't quite open completely. I have a hard time imagining why anyone would want to have their way with a woman that looks like me.

Still, store policy dictates that I lock up during the thinnest hours of night, and that I conduct any business through the double-glassed teller's window, a waist-high drawer that can be reached (even sitting down) from inside the small, Plexiglas cubicle we call "The Aquarium."

I noticed the truck when I happened to look up from "Surprising the Pants Off Him," an article detailing the extremes some women have gone to to spice up their sex lives, some of which was pretty unbelievable, like the woman who claimed to have met her boyfriend at the door wearing nothing but whipped cream. Needless to say, I was a little surprised myself when I saw the vehicle sitting beside the pump because I'm typically more observant. *Uncanny*, Harold says. I can be cleaning the coffee machine, my back to the window, and just know when someone pulls in. But this time I hadn't. Nor did I hear the register *bleep*, which it does whenever a pump's activated. No matter if you pay inside or out—cash or plastic—there's always a *bleep* when the pump comes on. So I looked at the panel and, sure enough, there was no light lit for number five. The guy had pulled up, but he'd not yet pumped any gas.

I first figured he was trying to work his credit card out of his wallet, or, as I've known some night owls to do, dig through the change they've dumped into the map-holder of the armrest between the seats, trying to find enough quarters to buy a gallon or so and get themselves home. Or half-drunk, mining for bills in the front pocket of his jeans. Or maybe just trying to remember why he'd stopped. And I say *he,* not because I knew it was a guy just then—number five is on the near side of the middle island, which is beyond pumps 1 and 2 and so mostly out of sight from The Aquarium—nor could I make out anything from our lousy security camera, which showed only the grayish reflection of fluorescents on the truck's windshield. Still, odds were that it would be a male, given that time of night. Like I said, some single guy on the way home from the bar. Or a salesman getting a jump on the miles that separated him from his first client of the day. Or maybe someone from the third shift at the bottling plant was getting to work late or getting off early. They're mostly men. Women have less reason to be out at that time.

The tags were Michigan, standard blue-and-white plates, nothing unusual. And it wasn't a vehicle I recognized—we do get a few regulars now and again—though the truck couldn't have been more ordinary. Just a white late-model F-150 Club Cab, like the dozen or so Fred Wheeler had lined up in front of his dealership during the Summer Closeout Sale. Around here, the driver of such a vehicle could just as well be a realtor or doctor as he could be a farmer or contractor. Could, I suppose—now that I think about it—even be a woman. Though in this case it wasn't.

I watched for about five minutes. When no one got out to pump gas, I began to wonder if maybe the guy'd fallen asleep. Maybe that's all he'd wanted—a safe place to catch a few winks so he wouldn't doze off at the wheel as he headed north on 131, accelerating across the median and crashing head-on into a FedEx tandem or Walmart semi, the two carriers that most often hum along the interstate at those times at night when the traffic seems to read my mood. Back when I smoked, we had to take our breaks outside, behind the store, as far away from the pumps as possible, and I would stand beside the dumpster as long as I dared, listening, on clear, operatic nights, to the long-held note of *s-w-e-e-t-n-e-s-s* or *s-o-l-a-c-e*, or, when it rained, of *w-h-i-s-p-e-r-s* and *w-i-s-h-e-s*. Every so often, even after I'd come to expect it, I'd be startled by the sound of a truck drifting over the rumble strip—as if a loud voice suddenly said *w-o-u-n-d-e-d.*

Some long-term drivers learn to catnap in the night, in order to avoid cashing out, or, at the very least, the hassle of insurance claims and vehicle repair. I've had a few stop in before. Mostly they park against the building, so as not to block the pumps. But some like to stay in a more well-lit place. At that time of night, if we're not busy, it doesn't really matter to me where they park. So I began to think the guy in the white pickup was simply napping.

About then, a gray Stratus pulled to the far side of pumps 3 and 4, catty-corner to the white pickup. A guy maybe in his fifties, by the looks of it, stepped into the camera as he ran his card at the pump—a salesman, most likely, by the looks of the suit pants and dress shirt, though without a tie. Probably on his way home. I watched him pump $26.56 into the tank. Every so often he looked hard toward the pickup at pump five. Kind of stared at it. Once the Stratus guy retrieved his receipt, he walked over to the driver's side door of the Ford and seemed to be talking to someone. Then he came over to the night window.

"Any idea what's wrong with the guy in the pickup?" he asked. He slouched over the metal circular two-way that allowed voices to penetrate The Aquarium's glass. He looked tired. A stubble of gray beard made his cheeks glow whitish beneath the mercury lights. Behind his glasses I could see him squinting and blinking, as if his eyes were uncomfortably dry. There was a ruddy smudge of something on the front of his pastel green shirt, dried ketchup perhaps, no doubt from eating fast food while he drove.

I shook my head, pulling my face into what I hoped was an expression of boredom and disregard, which would prove that I was not about to be bluffed into doing something stupid, like going out to see what the problem was. Maybe, it occurred to me, these guys were in cahoots, and were hoping to lure me into unlocking the door, making myself vulnerable. "No," I said. "Why?"

"He seems to be crying," said the smudged shirt.

"What?" I said. I wasn't sure I'd heard him correctly.

"He's crying," said the man, louder. "You may want to have someone check on him." He turned and walked back to the pickup. For a moment he stood at the driver's door like he was talking to someone, asking questions, all the time his hands flexing in the air, waving gently, the way Reverend Maitland's used to, during prayer, as he pleaded for our understanding. Finally, the Stratus guy dropped his arms, shuffled back to his car, and drove off.

And just who, I asked myself, *was the* someone *the guy expected me to have go out and check on him?*

I waited another ten minutes or so, assuming that the guy in the pickup would eventually get control of himself—if he was in fact crying—then take care of his business and be on his way. I considered several scenarios in the meantime, not the least of which allowed for the possibility that the guy was injured in some way, even dying. I considered calling 911. But the Stratus driver hadn't given any indication of trauma. He hadn't suggested that there was any emergency. No evidence of foul play. And I didn't want dispatch to make a big deal out of nothing. Still, after about ten minutes, I decided something else needed to be done, so I flicked on the intercom and tried to find out what was going on in the white pickup.

"Good morning, Pump Five," I said, in the closest thing I have to a cheery voice. "Do you need any help?"

The camera aimed between the two pump islands showed no evidence of movement.

"HELLO?" I said. "Pump Five! Are you okay?"

Nothing. I tried the intercom from pump two, opposite to pump five, figuring that since it was facing the driver's side of the pickup he'd be more likely to hear.

"HEY, WHITE PICKUP!" I shouted. "WAKE UP! ARE YOU OKAY?"

There was no reply.

More minutes passed. I returned to page ninety-two in *Cosmo* but couldn't concentrate. The compressor above the dairy case thrummed to life. That's when I began to consider other options. I could do nothing, of course. Wait until the next customer came in and see whether he said anything. It was just past three-thirty. Surely I'd have another customer within an hour. If not, it wouldn't be more than two hours before I'd have coffee made and be reopening the door. At six, Marj would be in, and whichever one of us went out to read the pumps could find out what the deal was. Or I could call the cops and hope that Doug West wasn't on duty. Doug was not a person I cared to see. Or I could call Harold at home, which he'd often told me to do if I'd ever gotten into something I couldn't handle. *As if!* I had no intention of disturbing his mother, who Harold had recently moved into his daughter's room, now that Beth's married and lives in Louisiana.

Or I could go out and check on the guy myself. As I said, I'm no lightweight and surely not timid. I've been trained in martial arts. What harm could possibly come to me if I left The Aquarium long enough to stroll out to number five and check on the driver of the white pickup? What if he really was in trouble? Injured? Having a heart attack? How could I live with myself if I just let the guy die sitting in a pickup by pump five, knowing that I could have done something?

We have a small Louisville Slugger behind the counter. It's the size of a police stick, only thinner, a child-sized replica of the real thing—a souvenir of Harold's visit to the Louisville factory and museum a few years ago. I thought at first that I would take the bat with me when I went out to confront the white pickup, but on second thought I decided it might appear too threatening. I wouldn't want the guy to react violently. Too many of these late night travelers carry guns of one kind or another. I didn't care to read about myself in the paper—again—from a hospital bed. It would be better to approach the truck casually, and so I took a clipboard with me instead, as if I was going out to record some numbers from the pump.

I unlocked just the Enter side of the doors and made my way to pump 1. From there, I could see a man hunched forward in the driver's seat, both hands at the top of the steering wheel, his head leaning against them. But he wasn't asleep. Nor was he dead, thankfully. Instead, his whole body was shuddering in spastic heaves—sort of like an epileptic seizure—and I began to review my knowledge of first aid, thinking *Why does it always happen to me?* I stopped beside the towels and windshield wash, double-checking for the squeegee—a possible weapon. It was then that the man in the F-150 turned to face me.

Sure enough, he was crying. He was maybe my age—early thirties—though his puffy face and wet eyes made him look older. He was clean shaven, with well-trimmed hair—brownish, it seemed, though I couldn't tell for sure, given the light—and if he wore glasses, he'd removed them, so as to wipe his rush of tears on the sleeves of his t-shirt, which he did every so often. And every so often he'd pinch both eyes with the thumb and index finger of his left hand, revealing a simple wedding band.

I moved a little closer—to see as best I could into the cab but still out of reach. I paused midway between the islands, a short dash to safety if I needed it, and I shouted at the driver's window: "Sir, are you okay?"

He looked at me, formed what seemed to be the best smile he could from a face that was being brutalized by sobs—a childish, pathetic smile—nodded ever so slightly, and then appeared to wave me away with his left hand. Snot was running from his nose to his upper lip. Without so much as a word, he hunched back over the steering wheel, his shoulders shuddering.

There is nothing uglier than a crying man, it seems to me. It's disgusting. There's little that compares to the sloppy, grotesque effrontery of male tears. Even at my worse, in fact, even shortly after the accident, when I looked at myself in the mirror for the first time, and I knew that my life as I'd known it was over, that I would from that moment on be a figure of darknesses and shadows, of third-shift employment and post-midnight shopping at twenty-four-hour Walmarts—even then, when I looked more hideous than any person deserved to look, I still would have won a beauty contest among crying men.

"Is there anything I can do?" I shouted. His head, resting on his hands, seemed to rock from side to side. "Do you need gas?" I asked. Again, his head rocked.

A dark van turning in off Perry Street made me return to the building, locking the door behind me. Oddly enough, it was a woman this time. Forty-ish. Jeans and sweatshirt. Short, tight hair, no effort to hide the gray. Someone's mother. She stopped her Honda at number three, the pump closest to where I sat behind the pay window. She ran her card, pumped thirty-one dollars exactly into her tank, and drove off. She'd paid no attention to the white pickup.

After a few minutes, when there was no sign of any other customers, I went back out.

"You can't just sit here," I said forcefully, trying to project decisiveness through the driver's side door. Any hesitation I had had up until then, any fear—any sympathy—was quickly turning to anger. I didn't know what this guy's problem was, but I didn't like the idea that he was making it a problem of mine. "If you don't need gas," I said, "go park somewhere else." The man gave no response. I tried threatening: "If you don't move pretty soon, buddy, I'll call the police."

He did not comply. I had no choice but to make good on my threat.

Sure enough, Sergeant West was one of the two officers sent to investigate my call. I didn't recognize the other one—younger, probably a new recruit. When they drove in, silent but flashing, they positioned the patrol car so it blocked the white pickup, and they left the doors of their vehicle open when they got out. As they approached the truck, I could see that Doug had his right hand resting on his holster. With his left, he was making circular motions in the air, indicating that the guy should roll down his window. It occurred to me then to flick the intercom back on, and I could hear Doug asking the driver's side of the white pickup if the guy was okay. But the window did not roll down. Immediately both officers began saying something, but the intercom—the cheapest I've ever seen—garbled it. I couldn't tell whether they were talking to each other or to the man in the truck. Finally, they seemed to pause and listen. The officer who was not Doug walked around to the far side of the white pickup and opened the passenger door. Doug turned and made his way toward me. I knew he'd want my statement, so I unlocked the main entrance again and stepped outside. To maintain a slight height advantage, I stayed on the curb, just in front of a pallet of Bug Off! windshield fluid—half of the gallons a shade of blue like an aboveground pool liner and half the reddish-pink of embalming fluid (laced with antifreeze and good to forty below).

"So what's the story?" asked Doug, stopping an awkward four feet from the yellow curb.

"I don't know," I said. "Like I told dispatch, he's been there since about a quarter to three, and he seems to be upset."

"He's crying," Doug said.

"I know," I said. "I checked him out." We avoided looking at each other. Instead, we both seemed focused on the situation at hand—the white Ford F-150 beside pump five, Doug's partner at the passenger door, scribbling onto the pad in his hand.

"By yourself?" Doug asked.

"Do you see anyone else here?"

"Not very smart, Amy," he said. "You of all people should know better."

I couldn't tell whether it was genuine concern in his voice or a thwarted lover's repressed anger. Either way, the tone didn't warrant my reply.

It's true, I'd never told Doug about the pregnancy. I suppose I felt it was my problem, not his. I knew from the start that the discovery of our relationship would cause embarrassment for both of us, a possible ethics hearing, maybe even sideline Doug's career. Still, at first, I didn't do anything to prevent it. I thought I was in love, and, at the time, that was all that mattered, especially as our love was so easily concealed. We were trained to be professionals; at work, we acted professionally. We appeared distant, even cold to each other—not unlike the way our conversation was going just then, the two of us staring at the white pickup. *Just the facts, ma'am.*

But a pregnancy is not something you can hide for long. A professional decision had to be made. And I made it. *Ancient history.*

"New guy?" I asked finally, as a way to help maneuver us out of what had become more than an uncomfortable pause.

"Been with us maybe six months or so," Doug said, without looking my way. "Charlie Temple's cousin. Remember Charlie?"

"Yeah," I said.

Charlie Temple's cousin closed the passenger door on the pickup and made his way to where Doug and I were staking out our former-lover's distance. He was blond and twenty-ish, with a narrow face and a pointy nose. He was grinning like he'd been in on some kind of practical joke.

"Do you believe that?" he said to Doug. "The guy's just sitting there blubbering. Won't say why. Says only that he'll be okay in a few minutes."

"But he's been there since three," I said.

Doug looked at his watch. "That's a pretty good cry," he said.

"It's un-frickin'-believable," said Charlie Temple's cousin, with a snorty laugh. "So whatta we gonna do? I mean, is there a law against crying?"

"No," said Doug. "But there is one against loitering, if Amy here wants to call it."

For the first time since I'd stepped outside, I looked at the sky. To the east, a faint gray tinge of light promised morning. It had been cloudy when I'd driven into work, the darkness close and thick, but now I could see half a sky of stars. The low pressure seemed to be moving on.

"Maybe a person just needs a good cry once in a while," I said.

"Maybe," Doug said.

The sound of the pickup's starter made Charlie Temple's cousin turn around. We watched as the pickup slowly reversed, far enough to be able to then pull forward around the open doors of the patrol car. At the end of the drive, its headlights flashed on and the right turn signal blinked. Then the white pickup turned right and disappeared in the direction of the freeway.

"How about that?" the new guy said.

"Son of a bitch," Doug replied.

"Son of a bitch," I repeated, under my breath. I'd never told him about my visit to the clinic either, about the way the doctor rested his hand on the inside of my thigh—even through his latex gloves, I knew he meant to be tender—or about the reason for my absence from work, the medications that would surely have shown up in a random drug test, the guilt of taking our baby's life. After that, I didn't much care anymore about police work, about Doug, about my own well-being. What I had done was, some believe, akin to murder, and I fully expected to be punished for it.

That's when I began to be reckless. That's when I started making trips out of town, to bars where I wouldn't be recognized. That's when our relationship ended. And that's when Sgt. West, the first on the scene of an ugly rollover along U.S. 131—on an early morning not unlike this one—discovered my mangled face in the wreck.

The Small Bridge

(

A young man in a red corduroy jacket stands near a small wooden bridge that he'd built himself and placed over a creek, or what he liked to call "the creek"—a rough, twig-lined trench the depth and width of a shovel, which, truth be told, didn't actually require a bridge, given its meager proportions, despite its serving as demarcation of one garden from another, and given that it barely filled with water but twice a year, spring and fall. Just now the creek was dry, unseasonably so for late October, as by all other reckoning it should have been afloat with yellow leaves of soft maple, with tarnished oak and gray-tinged willow leaves. But autumn had been droughty. And although for the most part the drought had suited the young man just fine, serving his predilection for bicycling—he'd passed many glorious afternoons pedaling the sun-stalled back roads of the county—just now he wished for rain. There was something sensual and promising about rain, especially autumn rain, and as he could see beyond his small bridge a tall young woman standing ankle deep in brown and yellow leaves, at pause from raking, he bargained with whatever gods might be available for a slight rain, for whatever possibilities might present themselves in rain.

Let's call him Will. For although his parents had prided themselves on the careful and deliberate selection of a given name for their first child, the young man had come to accept the fact that he would be known simply as Will, the single syllable reduction of a patronymic that was not difficult to say but was more unusual than his classmates or teachers had been comfortable with. He'd eventually grown tired of correcting them, of their inconsiderate disregard as to his preference for his ancestral birth name; in the end, he'd come to tolerate their abbreviation.

In opposition, as the framing of our narrative requires, the young woman standing beyond the small bridge shall be named Joy, apropos of her mother's exclamation upon the announcement at birth of the child's gender. Had Joy been privy to Will's thoughts not moments before, she'd now be contemplating her good fortune, in that not only was her name irreducible, but it was quite accurate in describing, in Will's estimation, her *being*. As corny as Will himself knew it sounded, he had been repeating to himself: *A Joy to be around.*

However, if Will had known what Joy was thinking, he'd have to envelope himself in the odor of autumn leaves and would have to remark how often that punk was accompanied in no small degree with memories of the lake cottage her family had owned when she was a girl. It was an attractive smell, in a way, despite her certain knowledge that what wafted from her raking was no more than stench of death and decay; it engaged a musky sweetness nonetheless. Toadstools. Leaf mold. Wood smoke. Bloom rot. For Joy, it was also the smell of sex. For the smell reminded her of weekends at her family's cottage, and of one particular day, the day when she first caught scent of a boy's sad semen, felt it sticky on her hand and wrist, first let a boy's finger probe the musky closet of her gender. Every autumn since has held at times for her moments of punky sensuality, the scent of late sun and yard chore perspiration, of wormy, rich compost and frost-turned gardens, of hollow insect carcasses, and fallen pears so rotten even the yellow jackets ignored them.

Yet unlike the young man across the bridge, who might have been wishing for some enlightenment as to the unspoken musings of his raking partner, Joy would not be thinking of the person who shared the scene presented here, but of a former love, of a former time, which she often did in autumn, which autumn often caused her to do. She knew Will was there, of course, across the small bridge, or what he'd called a "bridge," though the term had seemed somewhat silly to her, in that the step she'd taken to cross the small ditch, which (he'd claimed) occasionally filled with water, had not been much larger than her *pas de curb*, a movement one former lover called a *sidle*, like that of a dancer making her way after rehearsal to the open door of a waiting car.

But poor Will couldn't possibly know what she was thinking. He'd like to have thought that she was thinking of him, as he stood near the bridge he'd built—the bridge he'd told her he'd built—the bridge that bridged nothing, really, except a small overgrown ditch he called a creek, which was seldom creek-like, seldom running with water. It was more what the Nature Conservancy termed an "intermittent stream" (in the newsletter he periodically received), even though he was fully aware as he stood there, at a time when the creek should have been flush with rainwater and afloat with navies of leaf-fall, that it was simply a trench, separating the straw-like stalks of bee balm from the last gasp of fern and the ruddy heads of some flower he could not recall the name of.

Certainly, if Joy had been thinking of Will, and not of Michael, the boy from her past, and his family's A-frame cottage down the shore from her family's gray clapboard, and wondering where he might be at this very moment—if he was in fact divorced now, as she'd heard he was, or if she could possibly locate him through an Internet search—she would be calculating how much raking they had left to do, and how many more tarps spilling with leaves Will would have to drag back into the pines near the fence before they were finished, how he wished it were legal to burn them instead, or how he wished he were more like his

neighbors, who would burn the leaves anyway, damn the legality of it, and how much longer it would be until he could warm
some spiced cider for her, and simply sit and talk to the woman
in the leaf-colored coat, who'd come, she'd said, simply to help
. . . and what he might say.

What should be said, instead, is how very little they knew
of each other at this point in the story, how they had met only
recently and so had not yet developed the relationship that seven
months hence would generate a commitment, a marriage contract, and, slightly more than a year later, a child. Nor can it be
said what the child might be thinking about the two of them,
standing on opposite sides of the small bridge, as they would
be at some distant time, a time when the child, a girl, would be
occupied with stirring the yellow and reddish leaves that surfaced on the small pond which the creek emptied into, or *would*
surface from, had there been enough rain to form a pond, stirring the leaves with the dead willow branch she'd found in the
yard and turning over the dry, beached canoes of tree-drop and
imagination, all the while singing softly to herself a song she'd
learned at day care, a round, rowing merrily, and wishing for
water, for the playground a pond offers to a solitary child left to
her own amusements. She has yet to be named, of course, as she
is yet to come into being, given the time of our story, and yet it is
possible, now that we have placed her here, to consider what she
might have been thinking as Will (her father-to-be) and Joy (her
mother) stood at odds on either side of the bridge her father had
built himself and placed over what he liked to call "the creek,"
though it seldom ran with water, for if it had, the water would
have emptied into and become the pond that she was intent on
stirring.

Her name will be Artemis, given her mother's one-quarter
Greek ancestry and a somewhat odd, renewed interest in mythology that burgeoned during the months of her gestation,
a name that would eventually be reduced to the more familiar
Missy by her classmates and teachers, by her boyfriends and,

ultimately, by her husband—though that comes later. For now, she is four, maybe five, and she is stirring the dry leaves of what should be a small pond but is, in fact, nothing more than a hollowing out at the foot of a willow, an earthen bowl of leaves and twigs and, she discovers, a faded, half-page of some lingerie catalog, which, despite the discoloration, nevertheless reveals a woman that would for years to come represent what beauty a girl named Artemis deserved. It is a moment she will recall periodically through her adolescence and early womanhood, a moment that, in correlation to her own beauty, will fade as her name fades, as she comes to accept the more earthly looks of someone called Missy. Had she known then, crouched beside the pond, stirring the refuse of autumn and wind, that the woman in the lacy red push-up bra and matching low-cut panties, the stunning woman in the faded scrap of catalog, bore as her given name the name *Missy*, the child's life may have turned out differently.

As it was, Artemis was not thinking of her future mother or father, the two characters in our story who we've left standing on either side of the small bridge, years before she was crouched beside the pond and merrily singing to herself the song she'd merrily learned earlier that week at day care. Nor was Joy thinking of Artemis, or even of the likelihood that she and the young man who stood beside the small bridge, the bridge he'd built himself, would couple and bring into being a child, a girl child, and name her Artemis, and that she would come to abandon that name over time, abandon, as it were, her place among goddesses. And while Joy was in fact thinking of sex, it was more earthy and physical, more a consequence of autumn smell and memory than of childbearing, which did not, as we have seen, include, just yet, Will.

But if she had, if, instead of pondering over Michael, Joy had been able to know what Will was thinking, she'd have known how beautiful he thought she was, and how he thought fortune had come to him as from the benevolence of some god whose name he did not know, as if love were a kind of lottery, and though he had not bought a winning ticket, he had done something along the way that made the god that fixes lotteries smile on him and present to him this woman, Joy, standing ankle deep in leaf-fall, not to mention her blue Fisher touring bike, the two of them a most recent addition to the cycling club Will sometimes rode with, and who shared, he would discover later, many of the same interests, including each other's company, and that both would be able

—at least until their child, Artemis, was fourteen, and something would happen that would spin memory into a whirlwind of should-have-knowns, which could be traced as far back in time as the day a young man in a red corduroy jacket stood beside a small wooden bridge and contemplated what it was that held the attention of the young woman across the bridge, at pause from raking—

that both would be able to form not a perfect union by any means, but one in which each partner was able to overlook the small imperfections of the other, those small imperfections that, like small bridges, are better left unremarked.

All that remains, then, is for a slight rain to fill the air, as it soon does, and while no more than a thick mist, really, it is enough like rain to embolden Will, as if twice blessed by gods, into stepping across the bridge and drawing the young woman's thoughts to him by taking her into his arms and suggesting that the wet leaves will be too heavy to work with any longer, given the rain, and they should go inside the house (the house that would eventually become *her* house, the house that would be granted to her in the divorce), the house where Will was soon heating spiced cider on his stove and where Joy would be entertained for several years by his astonishing knowledge of topics she thought she was interested in at the time, like hunting and the moon.

The Pleasure of Your Company

Marla described the dinner as "our turn to entertain." But I didn't see a need to take a turn. Yes, we had been to John Foster's twice, during our first year in North Bank. We had attended his Christmas gala in December and then the pig roast and beer bash in July. Yet neither time did I come away feeling some obligation to repay his hospitality. Instead, I'd already had about all I could stand of John Foster.

Marla herself had sent out the invitations to the Christmas affair. It had been one of her duties as the most recently hired paralegal at John's office. She'd figured everyone of significance in town had been invited, if the sheer number of envelopes she'd addressed indicated anything, and so when John instructed her to add us to the mailing list, Marla thought it would be a good opportunity to introduce ourselves. Yet despite the hundreds of envelope flaps her sponge moistened, few people actually showed up for the festivities. And for good reason. John seemed to organize parties for the sole purpose of embarrassing any members of the community he was feuding with at the time.

At the Christmas gala, for instance, a five-foot-tall inflatable phallus, decorated with tinsel and lights, stood beside a half-ornamented artificial evergreen. Against the erection leaned an oversized gift card that read "To the Zoning Board." Apparently, Christmas happened to come the month after the board had re-fused a rezoning request by a construction company John had had an interest in (though the story was never clear if the inter-est was financial or amorous, since the company was in large part managed by John's girlfriend at the time). He ribbed me at the party and asked if I thought he'd gotten his "point" across, and I forced a laugh—more for Marla's sake than his.

The pig roast at the Foster farm in July featured porcine cari-catures roaming among the guests—we were supposed to guess which local figures they mocked—as well as an opportunity to "Kiss My Ass" (that is, pucker up to John's mule), an unplanned mud-wrestling competition, and a karaoke "roast," dur-ing which suggestive song lyrics were dedicated to prominent townspeople (most of whom were noticeably not in attendance).

Needless to say, I began to find excuses to avoid John's invita-tions, though Marla did represent us once at a banquet John ca-tered after he'd won a sizable estate settlement. Otherwise, like most of the town, I'd wised up to John's amusements and made excuses to avoid them.

So when Marla suggested that it was "our turn to entertain," which meant having John over for dinner—hosted at our house and at our expense—I opposed it. Frankly, I didn't see any way we could possibly "entertain" someone like John, not to mention what he might do to our furnishings. But Marla persisted.

"We'll *have* to ask him over eventually," she said, as she scraped leftover mac and cheese into the disposal. "After all, we *did* attend two of his parties." The earnest tone of her voice made me anxious.

"If you can call them *parties*," I replied. "There was hardly anyone there, and the few people who were did not look to be enjoying themselves."

"That's not the point," Marla countered. "It's the proper thing to do, to reciprocate invitations."

She was loading the dishwasher more methodically than I'd ever seen her do before. When I reached for the dishrag to wipe the table, she intercepted my hand with a refilled glass of wine. Clearly, she was serious.

"Do you think any members of the zoning board invite him to *their* houses?" I asked.

"I don't know," she admitted. "But Dannie has. And she said that he's not so obnoxious when there's no one around to impress—"

"—Or insult," I said. "And consider the source."

Dannie—Danielle—was a freelance court reporter who knew more about the county judicial system than anyone. She told wonderful stories about John's idiosyncratic approach to legal argument. Dannie, however, was somewhat of a character herself. She was medium height, thin, and built like a dancer; she wore leotards and pullovers mostly, even in court. Her hair—cut short, like Mary Martin's in *Peter Pan*—was a different color each time I saw it. Once, her streaks perfectly matched the orange shade of her Wisconsin Cheese sweatshirt.

"Besides," Marla said, "he's my boss. And we *need* my job."

"Oh, so *that's* it," I said, half-teasing, "a hostage situation."

She didn't smile. "It's not what you think," she said. Her tone of voice meant that the end of our domestic jousting was near. "He's got a new girlfriend and he wants to show her off."

"Let him take her to the roller rink," I said.

"You know what I mean, Michael," said Marla.

What she meant was that I had little choice. We soon negotiated a compromise that vaguely resembled an Irish peace agreement. Marla could plan a soiree with John and his new girlfriend, if Charlie and Dannie came along.

"I want witnesses," I said.

Charlie was Dannie's common-law husband. A likeable guy.

An anomaly for North Bank. When he wasn't substituting for the art teacher at the middle school, he was building a low-energy berm house out of unclaimed or unused materials that he'd buy piecemeal from wholesalers and recyclers in Grand Rapids. He laughed easily—mostly at Dannie's stories about John—and people around him tended to laugh along. His laughter seemed to well up from the depths of some uncanny sense of the absurd and issue forth from the lips one could barely see beneath the burning bush of his red beard. While I often assumed that Charlie liked John as little as I did, I also knew that Charlie and Dannie were among the few people who regularly attended Foster functions, what Charlie has been known to call "the best damn show in town."

Marla agreed that the six of us would make for a fairly balanced—if not manageable—evening, so we settled on one of the dates that John had suggested to her.

Yet even accounting for my willing capitulation, with a bow to conjugal bliss, regret clung to me like wet newsprint. I tried my Christian best to pardon John and his need for individual expression—what most people in town simply dismissed as a genetically engineered personality flaw—but the fact was I detested his arrogant wing walking, his clowning and showing off. To me, he was nothing more than a pompous, self-serving, over-inflated frog prince lording over the small pond called North Bank.

Nor did Charlie and Dannie help matters any when I stopped by their house to invite them. Their initial laughter was followed by the bandying of possible scenarios the affair would produce, punctuated by the recollection of John's past exploits, including the funeral of North Bank's longtime postmistress, where John's Richmond Brothers suit was complemented by a canary-yellow baseball cap that read SHIT HAPPENS.

"You gotta admit," Charlie said, "the guy's got balls."

"That may be," I said. "But does he have to act like he's the only one who does?"

"Are you jealous?" asked Dannie.

Her pixie smile suggested she was teasing, but I could never be sure with her. I considered the possibility. Perhaps part of my problem with John was me. To be honest, I don't much care for people whose activities could sell grocery store tabloids, and I cared even less that part of my job at the North Bank *Banner* involved editing stupid social notices in which John's behavior at certain fundraisers or blood drives was chronicled. John wrote most of the copy himself. Not that he'd ever donate any *money* to the cause—just his presence and notoriety. Apparently, that was enough for the townspeople of North Bank.

It was not enough for me. I saw right through him, having honed my journalism skills—truth and objectivity and all that— at the *Star* in Lansing, a city as flamboyant with small-town politics as any, not to mention rife with state-level panderers and buffoons. In my mind, it was all a performance on John's part, an act, and as much as he may have reveled in stardom, it was no more a show than a production at the community theater, so far off-Broadway as to be unworthy of even pursuing residuals.

Women, however, saw him differently. What women saw, according to Marla and Dannie, was the blond hair razor-cut to just above the ears, the strands of bangs falling boyishly across his forehead (which he'd sweep cavalierly into place with the index finger of his right hand, only to have them swoop again), and the blue eyes—the blue of stonewashed jeans—with a ring of white circling the pupils. He was built like a swimmer—broad shoulders, narrow waist—and his clothes were often tailored. Even in summer's casual shorts and a t-shirt, John Foster III looked like he belonged in an Eddie Bauer catalog. He drove women crazy— Marla said—crazy with desire at his manly attractiveness, crazy with frustration at his insensitive boyish pranks. And yet, he was seldom without. For every woman who gave up on him, there was another waiting for a chance to lounge in the passenger seat of his convertible . . .

Okay, I'll admit to some jealousy. But even accounting for that, I couldn't bring myself to like John any better, and I did not look forward to an evening of socializing with him.

Marla told John, "Cocktails at six." She'd planned a light summer harvest buffet for an hour or so later.

I told Charlie, "Five-thirty." To help get things prepared.

"You mean," he said, "to have a few drinks before they arrive?"

By the time the yellow Corvette pulled into the driveway at six-forty-five—"*So* fashionably late," said Dannie—the rest of us were on our second Manhattans.

"I hope this wasn't a mistake," Marla said suddenly, as she watched them disembark in the driveway.

"Too late to think about that," I replied. Yet, for her sake, I hoped the same.

John thrust a magnum of champagne in my hand even before I had the door wide enough for a person to enter. He was dressed as though he was the best man in someone's wedding—full tuxedo, including a silk top hat—and his shirt, a pastel pink, matched the color of his date's simple summer dress, a tight-bodiced affair with a knee-length ruffle. She could have been on her way to a square dance.

"This is Leslie," John said. "Leslie, this is Marla—my right-hand man."

Leslie's long hair was chestnut in color, and shiny, covering most of what otherwise would have been bare shoulders. The skin that did show—when she turned an ear toward whoever was speaking, a quirk I found quite sexy—was faintly tanned and lightly freckled. She had eyes the color of aspen leaves, sort of green-silver. Her smile could have clinched a beauty pageant.

Not wanting to give John any credit for good taste, I immediately dismissed her as a bimbo. In fact, I must have been dismissing her for a while because Marla finally said, "Let them in, for chrissake," and she pushed me toward the kitchen with the wine.

Leslie, it turned out, was no bimbo. She was a junior partner with an Ann Arbor law firm that specialized in domestic abuse cases. She was preparing briefs of some kind for a case before the Michigan Supreme Court. As an avocation, she sang for a '60s-style rock band that played fundraising events devoted to environmental issues. As a hobby, she collected baseball cards and player autographs. She even had a rare Pete Rose. She talked with animation; she was articulate and funny. As the evening progressed, I could tell that she was not only charming the pants off Charlie, but Marla and Dannie as well.

"Isn't she something!" Dannie remarked. She'd come into the kitchen to see if Marla needed help heating fondue.

"Who'd have guessed!" Marla exclaimed.

Surely not me, who was doing his best to play the proper host. I'd come into the kitchen to freshen drinks, but I suddenly felt queasy; I rapped the ice cube tray hard on the counter. *Why that jerk?* I asked myself. *Doesn't she know?* I was half-tempted to try and corner Leslie long enough to fill her in on what John was really like, but having noticed how naturally she'd rested her hand on his knee as they sat side-by-side on the couch, I probably had a better chance of drawing a bead on his blue eyes with a twenty-gauge.

I fixed myself another drink.

"How many is that for you?" Marla asked.

"Two," I said, and hurried back to the living room with my tray. I didn't wait for her correction.

Marla had gone all-out to prepare a light, elegant meal. There were cold vegetables—sliced carrots, cucumbers, zucchini—two flavors of vegetable dip, cream puffs stuffed with deviled ham, a couple types of fondue, seven shapes of crackers, three kinds of sliced cheese, champagne, and some special pastries that she picked up from the bakery. "It's informal," she kept repeating, as a kind of apology.

No one seemed to mind. In fact, no one seemed to even notice that everything had been set up on the table for some time, until Leslie finally asked, "Should we eat soon?" Only then did the rest of us make any kind of a move toward the dining room.

"Everything looks great, Mar," Leslie said.

"It sure does!" John raved.

I'd no sooner noted to myself how the compliment seemed to be out of character for John when it occurred to me that he had been exceptionally sociable and polite throughout the evening thus far, more reserved than I'd expected. As he steadied Leslie's plate while she enthused about the "many wonderful choices" she was hovering over, I began to wonder if I had been unfair to him, if I had misjudged him all this time. Maybe he wasn't the jerk I wanted him to be. Maybe Leslie could see something I couldn't.

The next thing I heard was a sound like the rustling of cellophane. At first, I thought a moth had gotten into the dining room and had flown too near one of the candles on the table. There was a small flash and crackle, then smoke. Suddenly, flames began climbing Leslie's hair as if it were a wig of thin fuses. She appeared to blaze. For a second, I wasn't sure what to do. I was standing directly across the table, near the cheese plate and fondue, within reach of her, but for some reason I couldn't move. Instead, I could only watch as the fire took flight, soared toward her lovely, cloud-like face—a face, I noticed, that now twisted grotesquely into an expression of fear and disbelief.

John was the first to take action. He began batting at Leslie's enflamed halo with his paper plate, flinging cauliflower and carrot sticks and dip across the room and fanning the fire in the process.

Dannie yelled Charlie's name. Charlie—a coolheaded exhelicopter gunner—pulled a cloth napkin from under the cream puffs, plunged it into the watery cubes of the ice bucket, and covered Leslie's head with it. At that point, Leslie screamed. Whether the scream was from pain or fear, or it was due to the coldness of the water, I don't know. All I know is everyone stood a good half-minute before we did or said anything. We stood and watched as Leslie sobbed beneath the wet napkin, her pink dress dripping with ice cubes and sloppy with blue cheese dip.

What followed was a communal sigh of relief—once we realized that Leslie hadn't been seriously hurt. The hair on one side of her head was blackened fuzz, her left eyebrow was singed to curls, and her neck was red—as though sunburned—but fortunately she had escaped any real injury.

What followed our relief was an overpowering stench of something awful burning—like smoldering plastic or leather. The smell, in fact, would linger in the dining room for several days. No one ate much after that. The evening settled into a coffee klatch of apologies and reassurances. After Leslie insisted five or six times that everything was indeed all right, that it was indeed an accident, that she herself hadn't noticed how close her hair was to the tea lights—we tried to make the best of it. Her graciousness and sincerity was sobering. She even joked about the "abuse" she was going to suffer at the office come Monday.

But while the women discussed possible hairstyles that would disguise the fact that anything had happened, the men tried not to look at her.

Not long after dinner, before Marla even had a chance to salvage dessert, Dannie and Charlie begged apologies and left—surprisingly early for a couple that had a reputation for lingering. I was sure it was a ploy to get John and Leslie to leave too, since I knew Marla was feeling horrible and simply wanted to get the whole evening over with. But for some reason, John and Leslie stayed behind, and we forced the small talk to silence. Finally, at Leslie's suggestion, we switched on the TV.

I must have had another drink while we watched the Tigers host the Blue Jays because what I remember next is kind of foggy. I hadn't wanted to look at Leslie too closely after the incident—I don't think any of us did. But about the seventh inning I glanced over at her on the couch. She sat to John's left. As before, she had her right hand resting on his left knee.

From his perspective, Leslie must have looked much like she did when they'd first arrived. Other than a few stains on her dress, the right side of her face had been left unscathed. Still, John was leaning somewhat awkwardly to *his* right, away from her, as though she harbored some terrible disease.

From *my* perspective, seated as I was on the extra chair we'd brought from the kitchen and placed to the left of the couch, Leslie could have been a twin to a freak in a sideshow—half woman, half alien—and when I looked at her sitting there, I began to laugh.

It may have been how silly she looked; it may have been some subliminal retribution for John's prior mistreatment of North Bank's well-meaning citizenry; it may have been the booze. But whatever the reason, laughter began to rise in me like champagne bubbles—fizzy at first, then warm and spurty. Then explosive. I began to laugh in great guffaws and I couldn't stop. I finally had to excuse myself to the kitchen.

The more I thought about Leslie and her ash-blackened make-up, and the more I thought about John's helplessness— fanning her brilliant head with a paper plate full of vegetables, a dumbfound expression on his face—the more I laughed.

Marla followed me. "Michael!" she hissed. "You're out of control."

"I know," I gasped. "Isn't it great!"

"Don't make things worse, *please*?"

"I'm not trying to, honey. Really! It's just—" But I couldn't speak. I found it all so terribly funny. I started to wipe my tears on the cocktail napkins and ended up giggling at their smoky, festive designs. I tried to fix another drink but found the ice cubes hilarious.

Marla went back to our guests.

Not two minutes passed before she announced they were leaving. I assumed enough control to say goodnight at the door.

"It's been *REAL*," I crowed—after they'd gone.

"Funny," was all Dannie said the next day, when I told her and Charlie about it. She said it in one of those polite, distracted voices that seemed to tender implication. Charlie just sort of shook his head, though I'm guessing his lips smirked behind his rowdy mustache. Still, I suppose it was one of those moments where you had to have been there.

Marla's forgiven me. She says it's not the worse thing I've ever done, and she's assured me that my laughing hasn't changed the way she's treated at work. Beyond that, I don't care. It was nothing I did. It was not my fault. If Leslie's feelings were hurt—or John embarrassed—then so be it. Call it karma.

Even the best lawyers can't argue that.

First Response

We'd been back from the warehouse fire about an hour—furniture, mostly, secondhand bedroom sets and so-called antiques, the kind that flash faster than scrub pine in a California drought, if you want to talk heat, or losses. The new kid, the one they call T.P., had already been cleared from the ER for the smoke he ate, and we were washing down the trucks for the second time that shift, when I suddenly thought about my first sleepover, or nearly one, and how I had the kid's mom call my dad to come fetch me. It was after eleven, and he'd already gone to bed. Still, in twenty minutes I'm back beneath my covers at home, and the next day Dad acts as if nothing happened, asks me if I had a good time.

I guess I'd been scared, though I always claimed *uncomfortable* when Sis started in teasing me about it, in those days.

He'd been my best friend. We'd hung out at recess, ate lunch at the same table in the gym, kind of gravitated to each other, often finding ourselves together, the last picked, for some game or school project. Must have been fourth grade. Funny that it'd come back to me then, of all times, washing down equipment. I hadn't given it a thought for years.

Does anyone know the real reason? Why I couldn't spend the night in that boy's room, a room he'd shared with his younger brother? What was his name? Kenny? *Kent.* Kent something. I don't recall the younger one's . . .

I was cold, is all. It was winter. The house was shabby and thin, with plastic sheeting in place of storm windows.

A week later, the younger one was dead. The boys had been playing along the Muskegon, on the ice—*river* ice, if you can imagine—and the way it was described in the newspaper, when my father read it aloud and asked me if it was the same boy, made me think of that movie *It's a Wonderful Life*, where the young George Bailey rescues his brother . . . what's-his-name. But Kent hadn't done any rescuing that day. Unless you count their hockey sticks.

His parents moved north shortly after, took him right out of school, to be closer to his mother's relatives. Otherwise, we might still be friends.

I pull forty-eights quite frequently now, seventy-twos when some family guy needs a sub. Doesn't matter to me. Sleepovers are just another part of the job.

A Real Deal

Lynnette loves linoleum. The words tasted bittersweet, like lemonade. She said it again: *Lynnette loves linoleum.* She inhaled deeply. *Lynnette loves the lovely smell of linoleum.* Her swollen tongue teased the enamel of her front teeth: *lovely, lemonade, linoleum.* She tried to recall what it had been like when she lost her front teeth, how funny she must have sounded. But it was years before.

Lynnette loves licorice. That's what the vinyl smell in the back store reminded her of. Especially the shiny black twisted licorice that Uncle Karl called "bike tires." Or the long, thin, stringy kind she and Jamie would buy at Lucy's and then lace into Chinamen's braids on their way to choir practice after school. *Lucy's licorice. Lucy's licorice laces.*

She missed candy the most, more than choir. But she missed school too. *Lynnette loves lessons.* She missed playing on the monkey bars with Jamie at recess. "Too risky," Uncle Karl had said. *Risky recess.* When her knees had begun to look like the maps that hung above the chalkboard—black and blue and green continents darkening pale oceans—Uncle Karl had said, "No more."

Every time she bumped her desk, she'd get another bruise. Lynnette *hated* it. She *hated . . . what*? There was no *h*-word for it.

Now she stayed home, waiting, often in the cool shadows of the back store, where she'd discovered among the long, dark skids of rolled carpet and linoleum a quiet place of her own. She'd pick her spot according to her mood—bright orange shag, cranberry Berber, imitation hardwood or brick—choose the best rolls to settle on, and she'd rest, or read, if there was enough light. She liked *The Babysitters Club*, and Nancy Drew, and those orphans—*The Boxcar Children*. After school, Jamie would bring her assignments home.

Jamie. Generous Jamie. Jamie, the jolly giant. Yes, all right. *Jamie the jolly giant jumps. Jamie the jolly giant jumps . . . giraffes.* She giggled. *Jamie the jolly giant jumps giraffes and juggles jam.* She'd have to remember that one.

Jamie was so lucky. She had Mrs. McLain this year. *Marvelous Mrs. McLain.* Lynnette missed Mrs. McLain, her favorite teacher, missed her fifth-grade classmates. The year before, when she had gotten so sick that she'd had to stay at U of M, every week the kids in Mrs. McLain's class made her get-well cards or pictures. By the time she came back from Ann Arbor, the bedroom she shared with Jamie was plastered with rainbows and unicorns. Somehow the kids in her class had known what her favorite things were, and she suspected Jamie.

You told them! Lynnette had yelled—as best she could, her voice still weak from treatment. It's not that she wasn't a little pleased, of course—even touched—by the gesture. But the big fuss wasn't necessary. She hadn't *wanted* to be sick; it just happened. She was no special person. Her mother had made that clear.

Jamie refused to take the cards down. "Too bad for you, Boo-Boo," she said. "It's my room too."

Surely, if anyone understood, it was Jamie, her cousin and best friend. Jamie had even stayed with her in Ann Arbor for those weeks last summer when Lynnette's blood thinned to Kool-Aid. They played about a hundred games of Girl Talk, and they sometimes slept in the same room at the Ronald McDonald House. Just like at home.

The Ronald McDonald House. What Uncle Karl called "the Golden Arches Grand Hotel," Jamie called "the Puke Palace."

"Where all the throw-ups stay," she'd said. On days when Lynnette felt good, she and Jamie made fun of the bald, plump, pale children, in spite of the fact that she knew—they all knew—there was no one sicker than she was.

Lynnette loathes leukemia. There, that was it. She looked at her watch. At school her friends would be in social studies, unless they were watching a movie. Today was—Thursday? Wednesday? What had Jamie said? Chicken fingers or pizza on the school menu? She couldn't remember. *It's either one more day, or tomorrow.*

Lynnette hated social studies, despite the *s*, its lisp and hiss. Uncle Karl called it "Dates and Deaths." Boring. Icky. Even math made more sense. *Math made more magic.*

Lynnette loves language arts, she said aloud. Oh those crazy *l*'s!

Lynnette loves lunch. It would be a while yet.

She leaned back between a pink crosshatched tile pattern and a gray-blue floral print. Suddenly she was tired. The back store was beginning to feel stuffy, even for April. So maybe all that ozone and greenhouse junk Mrs. McLain had talked about was true. Maybe the earth *was* dying. Wouldn't that be something? Maybe then, more people would learn what Lynnette already knew.

No, she couldn't wish that on Uncle Karl. *Kind Uncle Karl. Kind Uncle Karl cares. Kind Uncle Karl cares . . . about candy.* He'd said his sweet tooth was as big as a garage—a three-story parking garage fully occupied by chocolate Cadillacs. As big as Lynnette's sweet tooth even. Maybe bigger! She would never wish anything bad for Uncle Karl. He'd said it himself: "The best father money can buy!" And she thought so too.

The only father she'd ever known. For years it had been just her mother and her, and her mother never talked about her real dad. He'd not be someone to miss—not like she'd miss Uncle Karl. And her mother—well, she missed her mother, and *yes* she was anxious to see her mother again. Sort of. *Tomorrow, or the day after.*

It was in the back store that she felt the closest to her mother. Jamie and Lynnette had played there even before the Redi-Mix truck poured the floor. What had Uncle Karl called it? "The biggest indoor sandbox in the world!"

And after the cement was dry, after Jamie's and Lynnette's handprints and stick signatures were permanent—"like the Hollywood Walk of Fame," said Uncle Karl—but before the barn was stacked with rolls of floor covering and remnants, before the electric display wheel was installed, hadn't they had such a party—an open house—on her mother's birthday? Hadn't there been music and paper lanterns and dancing and laughter? Right there. Hadn't there been washtubs full of pop and beer, a plastic garbage can filled with ice?

"Yeow!" Uncle Karl had screamed, reaching for his favorite. "Frigorific!" Everybody laughed.

It was actually a word: *frigorific.* Uncle Karl was good with words, especially rhyming words. Not that anyone wouldn't guess driving past Karl's Karpets & Kollectables—or fail to notice the thirty-odd secondhand bicycles lined up by size along the driveway, from the twenty-six-inch Huffy at the front, down to the twelve-inch blue-and-white Smurf-cycle with the flowered basket. Behind the bikes were the dozen or so Western Flyers that she and Jamie used to ride down the slope in the yard.

But that was before.

Inside the former garage were Kollectables—flea market salvage—white glass dishes, canning jars, cast-iron lamps, antler tables, electric can openers, blenders, horseshoes, roofing shingles, bathroom vanities, and books.

"Another man's trash is Karl's treasure!" her uncle would sing as they scrounged yard sales and garages for worthy purchases. Some were *real deals*. Once he'd bought a push-type lawnmower from a man who'd gotten mad when the damn thing wouldn't start and so had gone out and purchased a new riding tractor. Uncle Karl replaced the spark plug for seventy-nine cents, cleaned out the filters, wiped off the grass and dirt from the housing, and sold the push mower for sixty bucks. "Total profit $54.21—not counting labor," he bragged.

Another time he acquired a complete library for eighty-five dollars, from a family happy to have someone "just cart the old books away." At last count, he'd sold four hundred and thirty-four of the books, including one leather-bound edition that a man from Lansing paid handsomely for.

Uncle Karl had tons of books—boxes and stacks and shelves of books—book club editions, condensed novels, biographies, paperbacks, and comics. Uncle Karl loved books; he claimed to own the store just for the books. Browsers would often find him slumped in the stained, gold-colored overstuffed armchair with the extra cushion (the springs were shot) reading a former best-seller.

"Karl and his books!" Aunt Ellen exclaimed, exasperated, her hands, filthy from gardening, pressed palms-out on her hips, like fins or small wings. She'd try to cover the ugly chair with afghans or quilts, to hide where the stuffing bulged like cattails, but dowagers who admired the handiwork tended to buy them right out from under Uncle Karl. His lack of interest—he'd barely look up from his reading—led them to believe he was hiding something special.

He'd put down his book only if the bell rang for the back store. The back store was Karpets.

When Lynnette once asked him why he didn't just own

a bookstore, he laughed. "No one will buy a used blender at a bookstore," he replied. "But lots of people will buy used books at a carpet shop. Especially if they think they're getting a deal. A real deal. That's the name of the game."

It was a game he liked to play, though his approach was more like checkers on a cracker barrel than the U.S. Open on TV. He played seriously, but he didn't seem to worry about winning every time. He simply liked to play, liked to barter; he liked the sport of bargaining and small talk, the society of commerce.

What he didn't like were the stuffy, mute collectors who sought investments—quick turnarounds, attic treasures, something-for-nothings—and mostly just circled through the store once and left. What he didn't like was "the old hi-and-bye."

Aunt Ellen, on the other hand . . . *Aunt Ellen enjoyed—Earth? Aunt Ellen enjoyed earthworms. Aunt Ellen enjoyed early earthworms.* She favored flowers. What else could be said?

Lynnette loves Ellen well enough. Funny vowels. And there were those l's again, loose and lippy.

Lost. Aunt Ellen at times seemed lost in thought. Like the week before, when Lynnette and Jamie were watching TV. During one commercial break, Lynnette caught her aunt staring blankly in their direction, embroidery motionless in her lap. Her eyes were dull, like a basset hound's. Not that she'd ever complained about Lynnette living there, about the drives to Ann Arbor for treatment, about Lynnette's laziness and unpredictable appetite. But there was a certain sadness to Aunt Ellen. An odd and obvious sadness.

Ellen gardens grandly. She spends so much time with her flowers! And they're all so beautiful! Like the yellow daisies she arranged in the Coca-Cola glass the day she told Lynnette about her mother coming. They were in the kitchen at lunchtime. And what had she felt then? *A hooray of happiness?*

No. *Sicker than sausage.*

Not now, Lynnette thought. *Now's not good.*

At the party, they had danced and danced. And the moths had spun shadows from the paper lanterns. And the fiddles and banjo had echoed from the woods, where the peepers sang along. Uncle Karl had tried to teach them a cowgirl dance. And they had laughed.

Then it was rock and roll, the radio tuned to "Golden Oldies," or something, and Mr. Watson—Mr. Bill Watson, petroleum engineer—had called long distance and dedicated a song to her mother—"Unchanged Melody" or something—and when the song came on, Uncle Karl woke them up so they could dance, though by then her mother's birthday was over. Lynnette had been so tired that it seemed like a dream to her, a fog. Like chemotherapy. Like she was ready to sleep for a long time.

But that was then and this is now, her stomach seemed to say. *Chicken noodle soup, if you please.*

Does she even know? Surely Aunt Ellen has told her. Or would her mother be surprised when Lynnette took off the cap and showed her. She kept what was left of her hair cut short above the ears, like Aunt Ellen's. "Easier to maintain when you're on the go," Aunt Ellen said. She meant the hospital. Yet unlike Aunt Ellen's hair, which was tightly curled and the chestnut color of the Oakdale floor sample in the display rack near the door, shiny and soft, Lynnette's hair was thin, blanched, and brittle. They'd tried to give her a permanent once, but clumps of hair came out in the process. That's when Uncle Karl bought the Tigers cap from Detroit, like Tom Selleck's in *Magnum, P.I.*, her mother's favorite TV show.

Without the cap, the only time her head wasn't cold was when Aunt Ellen gently massaged it between her hands. Lynnette would sit on the floor by the couch and lean her head onto her aunt's lap, both of them covered by a thick green afghan that Aunt Ellen had crocheted the winter before; then Aunt Ellen would ply her long, strong fingers across Lynnette's scalp and behind her ears, and the warmth of Aunt Ellen's rich earth would pass through to her.

So that would be it. She'd not wear any cap when her mother arrived, and Lynnette would know for sure.

Chicken soup. Chunky chicken soup. Lynnette smiled. *Campbell's Chunky Chicken Soup.* No, that would never do. *Chucky's chunky chicken soup.* Yes, more like it. *Chucky's chunky chicken soup . . . with chocolate.* Yuck.

So lunch then. Then a nap. And then Jamie would be home and they would work on assignments together. Lucky Jamie. Jamie'd have it so easy next year after helping Lynnette this year. She'd know everything already, even if no one's around to help.

They had danced and danced. She with her mother. She with Jamie. With Uncle Karl. Even after she began to get sleepy, she danced. And her mother had danced with her. And with Uncle Karl. And Mr. Watson had called from Africa or somewhere. And the song had come on. And her mother had agreed to marry him and go to him. And she'd danced into the sunrise. To Africa or somewhere, to be near him. Where doctors are scarce and hospitals don't treat leukemia.

Surely she remembers. Of course she does. Her only daughter. "I love you," she'd said. "It's only temporary."

And the moth-shadows fluttered about the paper lanterns, and the music had put her to sleep.

It would be lunchtime soon. Like the lunchtime when Aunt Ellen told her that her mother was coming. Lynnette was soaking a saltine to make it more palatable. "Like a raccoon," her Uncle Karl once said. "Lynnette the raccoon." *Raccoons rinse roast beef.* It had been a long time since she'd eaten anything like roast beef. *Raccoons rinse rare roast beef.* It would be a long time before she would want roast beef again. Mostly, she liked soup, though it tasted like bathwater.

And will he come with her? she had asked.

"Of course, honey. They're married now." Aunt Ellen had Lynnette's mother's eyes—brown and deep-set. But too close together for her face; she didn't have Lynn's more natural beauty. "A real looker!" Uncle Karl had once said, when she'd asked about her mother. Then he'd swiped a celery stick from the cutting board. When Aunt Ellen raised her wooden ladle near his head, he quickly added, "Like her sister."

Why shouldn't Lynnette be happy about it? At first, maybe. She missed her mother. But looking at herself in the bathroom mirror after lunch that day—without the cap—she didn't want her mother to come. Not now. Not like this. This was not *Lynn's lovely Lynnette.*

"I'll be okay," she had told Aunt Ellen. But she knew she wouldn't be okay. She didn't want any soup after that, the cracker fat as a dumpling. She hadn't felt well.

For the first time in weeks, her nose bled that afternoon. She must have wiped it with her hand and then brushed the wall while she slept. The wall was dull with blood when she awoke. And her joints seemed stiffer, more painful than usual.

But that was then.

Lynnette loves her mother. No. That would never do. *Lynnette loves Lynn,* her only mother. The mother who left her.

So a nap after lunch. Then Jamie would be home. But today she didn't much feel like doing lessons. Maybe they'd watch that kids' show on cable instead, the one where the point was to get as messy as you could.

"Tomato juice in your hair," Jamie said. "Gross. I wouldn't do that, not even for ten thousand."

"Me neither," Lynnette said. Just watching made her ill. Not the mess so much as the running and slipping and bending and throwing. She felt exhausted afterward. Still, it would be better than schoolwork, better than looking ahead.

Maybe just broth for lunch. And white bread, no crust. Or maybe she could skip lunch and just nap in the back store, in the dark, where the air was thick and cool, like Mammoth Cave. Wasn't *that* the best! Especially when the guide described the tuberculosis experiment and showed the rooms where patients actually lived for months, isolated and ignored. No outside contact. No fuss.

No one in Kentucky, no one above, even knew when somebody died.

Not like The Puke Palace in Ann Arbor.

They had gone on that vacation together, her mother and her. And Uncle Karl, and Aunt Ellen, and Jamie. Before her mother left.

Where there's little hope, the tour guide said, *one hopes for little things.*

"Little things," her mother repeated.

What if . . .

No, she *did* wish to see her mother again, to see her and to tell her how sick she gets just thinking about her. And how many times she wished for her mother to be there. Before it was too late.

Surely tomorrow, or the day after, when her mother finally returns, when her mother and Mr. Watson come from Africa to see her, to see how she is, when Mr. and Mrs. Watson come to visit their *lovely Lynnette,* their *dying daughter,* to see how much she's changed—surely it would be too late.

And it would serve her mother right.

And if she died between now and then? Her mother would expect to see her for the first time in sixteen months, expect to hold her and kiss her and to tell her how much she was loved . . . she'd already be gone.

Too bad for you, Boo-Boo.

Or, even better yet, like in the movies: Her mother comes in and finds her barely hanging on. And before her mother can take off her coat, before Mr. Watson even appears at the door, before anyone can say they're sorry, Lynnette will motion her mother close and whisper in her ear: *Have I got a deal for you! A real deal.*

Wouldn't that be the best! The old hi-and-bye.

Coda

Our final tune was always a Sousa march, like the one that goes *da da, da-da-da, da-da-da*—which Mitch Miller, if you recall, used as a sign-off for his sing-along show: "Be kind to your fine feathered friends . . ." I think it was Sousa. Always something loud and upbeat and meant for people to start clapping or pumping their arms like they were drum majors, eventually rising to their feet—a guaranteed standing ovation.

I played the trombone. Third chair, though there were only three in the pep band, so it didn't matter. We'd play at basketball games, pep rallies, and at least once every winter we'd pack up our instruments and bus over to the state hospital to cheer up the patients.

The place stunk. We'd be let in some unmarked service entrance and guided through narrow corridors—like we'd come in backstage to some grand concert hall—guards unlocking one steel door after another, locking them again behind us—to a room that reminded me of that crummy gym-slash-auditorium in the old primary school before it was demolished, but with thicker bars over the windows, and mangled cages securing the lights, half of which were never lit. We'd sit on unpadded folding chairs organized on the floor, since there were no risers, and use sheet holders instead of music stands—just to be safe.

We'd been cautioned: If one of them came onto the stage—which we found funny since we sat on the same level they did, on the same kind of chairs—we should just keep playing, as if nothing was wrong, and one of the attendants (that's what they were called, not guards) would come and help him back to his seat. *Him* because it was just men, every time, the place was segregated. I don't know who entertained the women . . . And they were harmless, mostly, we were told. Nothing to worry about.

Well, we had just begun the march—*da da, da-da-da, da-da-da*—when this guy in a grayish bathrobe comes right up next to me—I was on the outside, being third chair—and he begins mimicking my slide movements, marching around, smiling, then comes close enough to say something to me, though I couldn't hear, what with the trumpets and drums . . . He smelled like puke and urine, but he was smiling. Then off he marches, and I stopped playing to watch. He looked like he needed a good meal and a shave—his face had a kind of scruffy gauntness to it—but he was marching and playing his trombone with an enthusiasm I'd never seen before. He was really enjoying himself.

I'd played for five years by then. But I knew at that moment that I was done with it. It would never be anything more than a high school memory. I just didn't have the talent.

An Account in Her Name

The village hadn't changed much since I'd last been there. The campground was still wedged between the old railroad and the beach, though it appeared to be more suitable for RVs now than campers or tents. And the village park and public swimming area looked much as it did in its heyday, when it attracted enough tourists from downstate to sustain three short blocks of businesses along the shore of Crystal Lake. Or at least how I remembered it looked in the off-season. The white, sand-coated dock was gone, of course. As was the diving platform. But the swings near the bathhouse squeaked in a familiar pattern, and the tennis courts beyond the parking lot puddled in a familiar way.

The Beulah Drugstore looked much the same as well. I parked on First Street—where vacant spaces were numerous, as they had been thirty years before—and, for nostalgia's sake, I wandered in the side door and through to the front, passing bins of ten-cent candies, racks of comic books, shelves of plastic beach toys, t-shirts and hats that exclaimed THERE'S ONLY 1 CRYSTAL LAKE, and counters crowded with refrigerator magnets or Petoskey stones shaped to look like Michigan's mitten. It was a little eerie, in fact, trying to sort the current version of the place from my memory of when we hung out there as kids, drinking phosphates or hiding behind the magazine rack to read the comics without buying them. The only difference I could tell—beyond the tenfold increase in candy prices—was a liquor counter where the soda fountain used to be.

But the restaurant was gone. From the drugstore's front entrance, I could barely make out the building of my father's folly beneath the brown-shingled siding of the Benzie County Abstract and Title Office. The railroad tracks that once cut diagonally across Main Street, passing closer to the restaurant than the drugstore, were gone as well; in their place, a bike trail led eastward toward the old muck fields, which, by the waft of onions in the air, I assumed were still there.

For a moment I missed the place—the rattle of dishes when the coal train rumbled to Elberta with its cargo for the ferry. But the moment was brief. And it may not have been the place I missed as much as it was my sister.

The summer before my sister disappeared, she worked for the village of Beulah as a lifeguard and swimming instructor at the public beach. She had talked about trying to save enough money so she could study abroad her junior year of college—Germany, if I recall—and she knew that if she worked just for Dad she'd never see any hard cash. That she was able to do both—help at the restaurant and maintain her job at the beach—not to mention take care of her younger siblings—is nothing short of remarkable. But that's the kind of person Edie was.

Dad had had good intentions, of course. He'd bought the restaurant—one of only two in Beulah—upon negotiating the sale of Industrial Steel, the company he'd operated in Detroit since my grandfather's death. He'd envisioned the purchase of a "long-established family-style restaurant with prime location and faithful clientele" as a sure thing, a way of investing in a simpler—"better"—life for his children. In a single act of patriarchal responsibility, he relinquished the migraine of corporate presidency, eliminated what he'd often called the "certain heart attack" of commuting the length of Woodward Avenue six days a week, applied the equity from the sale of our Bloomfield Hills house toward restaurant refurbishment and equipment, and then moved the whole "fam-damily" north, where we crammed "temporarily" into my grandmother's two-bedroom cottage (with sleeping porch) on Platte Lake. Dad had planned to run the restaurant as a family business, providing his older children with employment and engendering in all of us good work ethics and responsibility.

But being that we were *family*, he seldom actually paid anything. Instead, he promised that our wages would be "reinvested" for our own good. He said that when we were three-starred in the *Michigan Travel Guide*—as he was certain we eventually would be—our rewards would be astronomical. In the meantime, we'd settled for our regular allowances and trusted in his careful tallies—some creative form of accounting that credited us with shares in the family stock.

Edie's wages from the summer before, for instance, had likely worked out to approximate the small percentage of her tuition at Kalamazoo College that wasn't already covered by scholarships and financial aid. Except for her tips—pocket money—she probably never saw any real earnings from the Main Street Restaurant. It was the reason she took on the lifeguarding job, which she eventually came to see as her primary occupation, despite the probability that Dad saw it differently.

For the longest time, I'd blamed *him* for Edie's disappearance. I was convinced that Edie had purposely run away, rejecting Dad's phantom dreams and fantastic expectations. I'd guessed that she'd bolted like a spooked horse from membership in a family she hadn't asked to belong to. For weeks I had refused to accept any other explanation. In my confusion and anger, I tagged blame like graffiti onto the first hard surface I encountered—the wall of my father's heart.

The distance from the drugstore on the corner to what is now a branch of Fifth Third Bank, half a block away, was shorter than I remembered. Yet as I entered through the thick glass door of the building, it was as if nothing had changed since I'd opened my first savings account at the Beulah State Bank, with the two dollars Aunt Sally paid me for washing her car. The whale's mouth of the brilliant brass-fixtured vault that as a child I'd thought was so beautiful gleamed ahead of me in a familiar, nostalgic way— like some kind of luxurious bomb shelter. For a moment I hesitated, dizzy from the sudden loss of years. Why was it so unsettling? A vault of such proportions was likely built-in, the walls raised around it, and so it would be unlikely, even thirty years later, that anything *but* a bank would be housed there.

My eyes had barely become adjusted to the change in light when a man came up and introduced himself as Jeffrey Castile, Branch Manager, whom I'd spoken to on the phone. I recognized the name; it was a family whose members were well distributed in the county. He was early forties maybe, though the color of his eyes seemed older, a likely consequence of tinted contacts or the fluorescent fixtures. Otherwise, he looked fit and established—a little too cosmopolitan for Beulah perhaps—but, after all, it *was* still a bank. And bankers were the same everywhere.

"I thought I saw the resemblance," he said, something I'd not heard in years. He looked at me as if I clearly was my father's daughter. A touch of his hand to my arm guided me into a paneled office, where he gestured for me to sit in one of the two chairs that faced a typical banker's desk, dark and uncluttered. Then, instead of settling himself into the large leather office chair behind the desk, as I had expected, he scooted up the twin to mine and sat beside me.

The polished desktop was bare except for an embossed coffee mug full of pens, a green, legal-size file folder, and a photograph of a woman and two children posed on a dock that looked
somewhat like the one I'd remembered at the public beach. In
the background of the photo was the faint suggestion of a Crystal
Lake sunset.

Mr. Castile—"Please, call me Jeff"—noticed my glance.

"It was taken the last season before the village board voted to
remove the dock," he said. "Quite fortuitous, don't you think?
That's my wife, Mary, and my boys, Eddie and Zack." Reaching across the desktop, he spun around and removed a stiff, per-
forated piece of paper from the file. "It's normally against bank
policy," he said, "but I've managed to keep the account active,
no matter what. It's the least I can do."

If Dad had been led to believe in the boom and hype of 1960
America—that good intentions would reap astronomical bene-
fits; that opportunity thrived in every village of the country; that
success was no more than *access*, an expansive highway system of
middle-class tourism and disposable income—he wasn't alone.
You only needed to turn on the TV to see average Joes—hard-
working and decent—rescued from poverty or economic pitfalls
by the largesse of a million dollars, simply because they were,
well, average and decent.

No one mentioned luck, that cruel god. No one said that even
the best intentions couldn't guarantee delivery, that delays were
also inevitable—like the Friday before Memorial Day when the
Gordon Food Service truck broke an axle near Mesick, and spaghetti had to be substituted for the seafood buffet. Belief alone
was as much as most people had, and Dad believed that eventually reward would swing off southbound U.S. 31, glide into town,
coast past the bowling alley and the A&P, cruise to the end of the
block, and pull up like a shiny pink Lincoln, polished and glitter-

ing, to the door of the Main Street Restaurant. For Dad, it was just a matter of time.

He refused to accept the possibility that luxury could be side-tracked, take a wrong turn and end up mired down some unmarked logging road in northern Michigan. He'd never accepted that something had to be said for a reliable, though secondhand, Ford Ranch Wagon. He'd never settled for the practical.

What all that meant for Edie, of course, was *work*. While her lifeguard job kept her free from the blue-striped waitress uniform most of the day, once she'd closed the beach, stowed away the ring buoys and first aid kit, swabbed out and padlocked the changing rooms, she'd hustle up the block, round the drugstore, and cross Main Street to the gray, flat-roofed, single-story, green-curtained building next to the railroad tracks, where she'd do whatever was needed during the dinner hour—seat customers or bus tables or make change at the register. Then, at the lull, she would herd into the banquet room those of us younger kids who weren't helping, and there she would see to our needs. As the eldest, Edie was responsible for making sure we got fed—especially during the Friday All-You-Can-Eat Fish Fry, when Dad was often so busy he couldn't have met a pink limousine at the door even if one had appeared. Later, she'd help him close up.

First thing in the morning, before she went down to wipe off the dew from her lifeguard tower, you would find her back at the restaurant, making what Dad advertised as "The Best Darn Coffee in Benzie County."

That summer was no vacation for her. And yet, to be fair to our father, Edie herself wasn't much into vacationing. Like Dad, she was driven by certain desires. She didn't place faith in serendipity, as he did, nor did she look too far ahead. But she would calculate what she thought she could accomplish in a few months, and then she'd commit herself entirely to accomplishing it. That way, she seldom fell short of her objectives. There were too many variables, she'd once told me, to estimate what she'd be doing years ahead. Instead, she'd only plan what she was capable of short-term. It was her way of avoiding disappointment.

And yet, if she imagined herself on a parapet overlooking the Rhine come the following March, you could bet that that's where she'd be. And if she planned to spend the entire summer earning money, there'd be no time for leisure, no time for after-dark hide-and-seek with her younger siblings. No time for bonfires or boys. She might have gone out at night maybe twice all that summer, to the Cherry Bowl Drive-In with my older cousins. More often, she would slip into bed not long after she tucked us in, claiming she was too tired to do any "goofing off in the dark."

For the rest of us—Tom, Jilly, Sammy, and me—summer mostly meant *vacation,* and the one drawback to Edie's course of action was that she approached her every task with the same no-nonsense, businesslike attitude, including her supervision of us.

What comes to mind now is the banquet room, a dozen tables separated by sliding doors from the diner-like counter and main serving area of the restaurant. Except for the one night a month when the Kiwanis met there, that's where we ate. The doors were just to the left of the small, glass-fronted gum and candy case where the cash register hulked, near enough so that Edie could collect receipts or make change and still watch over us at the same time.

"You will *please* remove your elbows from the table, Tom," she insisted at one meal, emphasizing *please* in a way that rendered it immune to negotiation. Her requests were often declarative.

Tom responded with the full authority of his thirteen-year-old hormones: "So who died and made *you* the boss?"

"When Mom's not here," Edie said, "I'm the matriarch."

"What's that?" asked Jilly. "Some kind of bird?"

"No, silly, it's a kind of *dinosaur,*" said Tom. "The extinct kind." He leaned forward on his elbows and smiled at Edie from the far end of the banquet table, where he'd isolated himself, leaving vacant chairs on either side. The rest of us were within Edie's reach.

"Not in *this* family," Edie insisted. The way she'd said it made it true. Tom excused himself to see if Dad needed help in the kitchen.

Edie was the closest thing we had to a parent that summer. Dad and the restaurant were indistinguishable. While some nights I heard him come home (well after we were supposed to be asleep), or some mornings I'd wake to his tap on our bedroom door and his whisper to Edie that "Time was awastin'," I mostly just caught glimpses of him through the serving window at the restaurant, his scrappy tufts of temple hair thrust like antennae in a swirl of steam or smoke, his high forehead glazed with sweat.

Mom was in Lansing most of the summer, taking classes at Michigan State, working on what she'd come to call "the degree childbearing prevented me from completing." To hear her tell it, the very day that Sammy, the youngest, got on the school bus for first grade—his first full day at Honor Elementary—Mom suffered a crying binge so horrendous she didn't think she'd be able to bake any pies for the restaurant. She didn't know what she was going to do. Then something happened as she was peeling apples—"something spiritual, a vision"—and she read the answer in the skins and cores in the sink. By late afternoon, when the school bus dropped off Sammy and the rest of us at the end of our road, Mom had already registered for as many courses through community education as she could.

For the first year, she juggled homework with housework and helping at the restaurant. But she'd felt her progress was too slow. Only one or two extension classes were offered at the high school each semester. At that pace, she'd said, her degree would be the death of her. But in the summer, with Edie home from college and our Aunt Sally—Mom's older sister—in her summer place just down the road, Mom was able to take a full load of courses. By staying in her old sorority house in East Lansing during the week, she could finish her degree more quickly, and so more quickly get a teaching job, which would contribute—in the long run—to the welfare of the family at large. Only on weekends—and then only if she didn't have too much studying—did she ever come home. Even then, she was often too busy with schoolwork to help Dad prepare meatloaf or to bake pastries for Sunday brunch.

"It's not *supposed* to be fun," Edie said once, when I asked her if she was enjoying the summer. "It's a *job*."

Edie disappeared one Friday afternoon in October on her way home from Kalamazoo. She'd phoned on Wednesday and told me to tell Dad she'd be coming, that she'd arranged a ride. Things were going fine, she'd said. She just wanted to get away from the dorm for a couple of days.

She asked how I was, how everything was going at school. She asked about Sammy and Jilly and Tom. I said everything was fine. I was the last person in the family she spoke to.

As far as I know, the police never had any leads. She's never been found. Nothing of hers—her driver's license, her birthstone ring—has ever turned up. She's never resurfaced, as from amnesia. No one in the family, as far as I know, has ever received even a postcard from her.

What we do know is that she had been to chemistry lab that Friday morning. Then she'd stopped by her dorm room and left her roommate, Jan, a note to the effect that she was all set to go home, that she even had a ride. But she'd never said with whom. The police never said if they knew.

Jan had been the last one to see her. Edie had seemed anxious to be going home for the weekend, Jan said, but they'd not really talked for a day or two, as their class schedules were opposite, and Jan—*who was sorry, so, so, sorry, so very sorry*—had been spending a good deal of time away from the dorm anyway, with her boyfriend Peter.

A week or so later, Dad went to Kalamazoo and brought back Edie's things. He said there didn't appear to be anything out of place—nothing wrong, nothing missing. Only Edie.

The restaurant failed the following year. Dad sold off the equipment that the new owners, who planned to open a bakery and catering business, didn't want. For a short while, he managed the office of the Frankfort Lumber Company. Then, later that same year, my grandmother died, the cottage was sold, and Dad was left with a small trust fund, enough so he wouldn't have to work as long as Mom was teaching. He retired early. When Mom got her degree, and a job with the Traverse City School District, we moved again.

We left Edie behind. We left her behind in the knotty pine bedroom she and Jilly and I shared that summer. We'd left her behind when all her college things were discarded or given away, when Dad stopped comparing me to her, and when Mom started calling Jilly her second daughter. I left her behind when I crumpled up and threw away the drawing I'd once made for her, which we found beneath the dresser at the cottage when we moved. It was a drawing of a road, a practice in perspective, which Edie had shown me how to do one drizzly and cool summer afternoon—a road that crossed the horizon somewhere in the middle of the paper, where two curvy lines came together in a point, and all along them the bright, scribbled curlicues that must have been trees—red and orange and green—and in the foreground a sign: TO KALAMAZOO.

It was during my senior year at Albion that Mom left for California. She said there was no longer a reason for her to stay in Michigan. Sammy was the only one still at home, and he was in high school. The rest of us had forged our separate ways, to college or the Air Force or marriage. I completed an English degree and then studied law at Wayne State. But I never took the bar. For over ten years now, I've been a legal research assistant in the claims division at Nationwide Insurance.

When Dad died, Mom suggested that I handle the estate, such as it was. Not because of my legal background but because I was the sibling who lived closest to the third-floor condo overlooking East Bay in Traverse City, which Dad had bought after Mom and Sammy moved away, the condo Dad always claimed had a view "worth dying for." One afternoon, his neighbors found him on the first-floor landing, where his heart had given out. He'd just come back from a walk on the beach.

Mom refused to fly in from San Diego for the funeral. She said it was a part of her life that she'd just as soon forget. If there was anything of value, we could divvy it up among us kids. Otherwise, I could do with his things what I thought best.

I discovered the bankbook in Edie's name while sorting through the paperwork from the restaurant years. The final deposit had been recorded in November of the year following Edie's disappearance—a full year later. But there was no record that the account had ever been closed. When I called the bank in Beulah—or what is now the result of various acquisitions and mergers—the branch manager, Jeffery Castile, told me that, over the years, my father had been sent innumerable notices concerning the account—notices about change of address, power of attorney, reinvestment, taxation, fund absorption—even notices sent registered mail. But Dad had never responded. He had chosen to ignore them, even as the interest compounded.

As long as I was in the area, the manager said, we should get together and discuss this. Could I drive over and meet him? And bring the bankbook, or any monthly statements I could find.

Jeffrey Castile lifted from the green file folder and handed to me a printed bank check payable in my name, for an amount I'd only ever seen on court-determined claims payoffs through my job at Nationwide. My mouth went dry. I didn't know what to say, or even if I could speak. It wasn't that a dozen questions didn't come to mind; I simply didn't know how to make my lips form the words. And then, just as suddenly, it seemed like an incredible emptiness sucked all the oxygen from the room. Like we'd been closed and sealed into the bank's magnificent old vault. For a moment, I couldn't catch my breath. A wild crying prevented it.

When I recovered enough to look up at him—seconds, minutes later—it appeared that Jeffrey Castile had been overcome as well. He struggled to speak.

"Your sister," he said, "saved my life."

While I surely must have given it some thought during the years since my sister disappeared, maybe even dreamt it, re-envisioned it, embellished it to the point of memory, it wasn't until Jeffrey Castile handed me a check for more money than I'd ever win in a lottery that the most vivid recollection from that summer resurfaced, even among the tears and blubbering that I could not control.

It was a mid-afternoon in August, a time when the beach would be busiest, given the hot weather. And I was hot in more ways than one. I was not happy about having to be inside on such an afternoon, setting tables and loading napkin holders before the dinner crowd arrived; I'd rather have been at the beach, where everyone else was. So I was surprised when Edie came through the door asking, "Where's Dad?"

A dumb question, I thought, and nearly said it out loud, for she knew full well where he'd be—in the kitchen preparing the daily special. Yet when I looked up to make some snide answer, I realized it was a good time not to. Splotches from a wet swimsuit soaked her cover-up, and her damp hair was plastered, flat and lackluster, against her face, making it look thinner than I'd noticed before. Her shoulders, muscled from weeks of swimming, seemed to droop unnaturally. She looked like a poor imitation of the confident, perfect sister I shared a bedroom and tidy closet with.

"In the kitchen," I said. I took a hopeful glance out the window to see if maybe it had begun to rain, forcing the beach to be closed early and returning all able-bodied youngsters to their families' businesses to help. But the sky was a cloudless pale blue.

There was obviously something wrong. I followed her as far as the front counter, pretending to get more napkins. I wanted to hear what she'd say to Dad, but I knew if I went back into the kitchen, he'd chase me out. So I stood as close to the server's window as I dared.

". . . diving . . ." Edie seemed to say. The noise of dishes being rinsed in the sink and the exhaust fan above the grill prevented me from hearing their conversation completely. I could tell only by the inflection in his voice that Dad asked a question.

Edie seemed to blurt out "Frankfort" and then I heard what sounded like a sob. But I couldn't hear anything else. There didn't seem to be any more conversation after that, or even any movement in the kitchen, though I knew Tom was back there too, washing dishes throughout the exchange. I eventually returned to my tray of silverware, knowing that Tom could not resist blabbing what he knew.

That evening, well into supper, Jilly asked Edie if she'd really saved someone. Until then, we'd all been unusually reserved— some of us because we knew something had happened; others of us because we'd sensed it was the right thing to do. Edie had said she wasn't hungry. But she sat with us in the banquet room anyway, the whole time we ate. She cut up Sammy's meatballs before he'd even asked, and she managed to ignore Tom's slurping a too-long spaghetti noodle.

"I don't know," she said. "I haven't heard."

Sammy began to giggle. He turned to me, his grin bright with treasure about to be spilled. "Lori," he said, "did you know Edie was kissing a boy today?" He fingered a piece of meatball into his mouth.

"It's called *resuscitation,* you dummy," said Tom. The length of the word seemed to edge his voice with impatience. "Life-guards do it all the time. It's like part of their job."

"Right," Edie said. "All the time. Now eat your dinner."

Sammy looked at Jilly across the table, gave her a smile. He whispered, "Edie kissed a boy!"

"Edie kissed a *bo-y*?" Jilly repeated, her voice rising into song. "Edie kissed a bo-y!"

As though on cue, Sammy joined her in a chant: "EDIE kissed a BO-y! EDIE kissed a BO-y!"

"Oh yeah," Tom interrupted, loud enough to be heard over the ruckus, "a real *boy*—about Lori's age." His tone was flippant, maybe even cruel. But he looked at me in an odd, pleading way, not typical for Tom, a way that suggested I should do something, as though the second oldest daughter—younger than he was, but more mature than the littler ones—should take command.

I looked at Edie. She was silent, half smiling, like she didn't want to make a big deal out of anything—like she didn't have the patience or strength to get upset, like it wasn't worth trying to explain something important to someone who wasn't able to understand. She looked tired.

"You'd better be quiet and eat, Sammy," I said, "or Edie won't kiss you goodnight no more." The tone of my voice surprised even me. Both Sammy and Jilly fell mute.

The rest of the meal was unusually quiet, though for some minutes Jilly sought Sammy's attention by giggling and making kissing noises with her lips. But Sammy ignored her. He poked idly at his spaghetti, as if he too felt something wasn't right.

As for me, the hair on my neck had begun to tingle, and I wanted to know the whole story.

Later that night, after Jilly and Sammy were in bed, Edie told Tom that Dad didn't need her at the restaurant, so she was going to Aunt Sally's for a minute, to call her there if there were any problems. The screen door had no sooner clacked shut before Tom roused us and told us what he knew. Some boy about my age had been showing off on the diving platform and had fallen awkwardly, striking his head on the iron legs—or he'd hit the water wrong—and Edie had had to swim out and carry him into shore and give him mouth-to-mouth resuscitation until the ambulance arrived. He was taken to the hospital in Frankfort.

Whispering in the faint light, Tom tried to downplay any possible heroics, but I could tell he was impressed by what Edie had done.

After a pause, Sammy said, "Tom, are we gonna be in that parade in Frankfort? 'Member, we dressed up like cowboys?"

"That was *last* Fourth of July, stupid," Tom said. "We didn't go this year." He seemed upset that Sammy didn't understand.

Sammy squinted his eyes and scrunched up his nose, like he was trying to think real hard. His face was gray from the last bit of sunlight that filtered through the screen. The boys were sitting on Edie's bed, the bunk below mine. I sat on the edge of Jilly's cot, facing them. Jilly had drawn up her knees to give me enough room, but otherwise she hadn't moved. She lay on her side beneath a single sheet. When no one said anything for some time, I began to think that maybe Sammy understood better than Tom thought. I wanted to change the subject too. I felt like I was supposed to feel sad or scared that the boy was hurt. Or proud of Edie for rescuing him. But, frankly, I didn't feel anything like that. I just felt kind of empty, like I was missing out on something.

Finally, Sammy asked, "Think we'll go next year, Tom?"

"Go where?"

"To the parade."

"Shut up, Sammy," Tom said. "And go to bed."

By the time I'd brushed my teeth and climbed into the top bunk, Jilly was already asleep, or pretending hard to be asleep, tucked in a cannonball near her pillow. She'd never said a word.

For the next couple of days, we stayed with Aunt Sally instead of going to the restaurant or the beach. Her boys were older and worked all day: John, at the grocery store in Honor; Mark, at the Platte River Canoe Rental. Aunt Sally showed us how to make tents out of blankets and clothesline. We fished off her dock. We learned how to play croquet. Aunt Sally was the one who told us the boy would be all right.

Edie appeared to be back to normal after that.

In Jeffrey Castile's office of the former Beulah State Bank, I cried in a way that I don't ever remember crying before, not even after Edie disappeared. I cried breathless, snotty sobs. I choked and blubbered. I dissolved the dozen tissues that a teller had brought me, and I soaked the better part of my sleeves wiping my eyes. I cried the whole time Jeffrey Castile described what he knew of that fateful August afternoon—or at least what he'd come to know about it later, after he'd gotten out of the hospital, after he'd learned that Edie had been the lifeguard on duty, and then what he'd come to know *much* later, years after she'd disappeared, when he'd taken on the management of the account in her name.

His hand rested on my arm. The touch was Edie's. He was sorry, he said, that it wasn't enough to show his gratitude. I assured him it was. We'd not have been there but for her.

What does it mean to save a person's life? At what cost? They were questions I hadn't asked myself in years. But on my drive back to Traverse City that afternoon, such questions filled the car like sullen hitchhikers. I recalled what I could of Edie and the summer before she disappeared. I thought of Dad and his restaurant. I thought of Mom and her need to get away—of all our needs to get away. And I was reminded of the times I'd asked those questions before, my own weak efforts to understand.

Summers during college I worked concessions at Cedar Point Amusement Park, near the swimming area, where I could watch the lifeguards, their good-natured reprimands and goofing around. Over the years, I even dated several of them. I seemed to be drawn to them, to tawny, broad-shouldered college boys, and at times I felt safe in their arms. But the relationships never lasted; too soon my heroes fell short of heroic.

When I would ask them about it, about rescues and resuscitations, most shrugged off my questions—humbly, I thought at first—until I realized that very few of them had ever *saved* anyone, that lifeguards are trained to prevent themselves from having to do so. Only one of the boys I dated ever admitted to a swimming rescue. A fat, stubborn adolescent girl (as he'd described her) had been washed off a sandbar as she was braving Lake Erie's notorious surf. He'd been stupid, he said; it was the only day he hadn't unchained the surfboard from the tower, since he'd thought no one in their right mind would venture so far out in such waves. He *had* to swim her in. And he'd fought her—and an undertow—the whole way.

"What was it like?" I asked. "How did you feel afterward?"

"I threw up," he said. "Grape soda in the sand—not a pretty sight."

"And the girl?"

"Okay, I guess. I never heard."

When I think of Edie now, I don't think of the beach at Beulah, of the Main Street Restaurant, or even of that summer before she disappeared. For some odd reason, I think instead of highways and restlessness, of the places we come from and the places we go, of interstates and distances, and, even more oddly, of my father's overwhelming desire for the things he'd never have—not just a three-star listing in the *Michigan Travel Guide* or a shiny pink Lincoln—but something like redemption, and the love of a daughter who knew he meant well.

In the drawing I made for Edie, the one we found beneath the dresser when we moved from Platte Lake—the one I'd thrown away—a road twisted upward, through scribbles of autumn-colored trees, to a point mid-paper, where the lines joined, cresting the horizon. I imagine now that two figures stand there—below the convergence but above the sign TO KALAMAZOO—one on either side of the road. The far one is my father. He's facing away, toward a thermal swell of asphalt, where the future is likely to appear, its riches destined for him. The other figure—the closer one—is Edie. She's staring at the road below my hand, near the waterfall of black crayon at the edge of the paper, studying every crack and pothole, certain of where she stands.

Look, I want to say. *Look across the road.*

Housekeeping

Not many guests leave tips these days, which is why I'll re-member them. A five-spot every morning beside the TV. And cheerful in a meaningful way. Not *Good morning!* as some kind of obligation. Honestly old school. Though mostly it was the woman, her face full of smile and a bright chirp to her voice, like a cardinal's on the first real spring day. No effort to it.

Even when they surprised me, coming back into the room as I was remaking the bed—I'd gone to see Francine for different sheets—they were super polite about it, almost as if *they* were the ones imposing. A nice-looking couple too, though he was maybe a few years her senior.

I could count on my fingers the real tips I've gotten here, in the decade I've worked for Hilton, though overall we're paid pretty decent, so I'm not complaining. And that's not count-ing the change left behind—piles of pennies and dimes—mostly, I think, to avoid problems with security at O'Hare. And every so often some elderly couple at the end of a lengthy stay might leave a stack of ones—guilt money for the discount they'd gotten through AAA or AARP. They'll have seen the room prices listed on the back of the door and worry that they're cheating Mr. Hilton out of his retirement. So they leave a little extra. Old school, as I said. Tipping's rare these days, even for those people willing to pay eighty bucks to see Donny Osmond in some kind of musical.

Still, anything's more than I got at the last place—I won't mention it by name. Eighteen years I cleaned those toilets, chlorined the love-spit from the sheets, lined up the melon shampoo, and for what? Washcloths stained with beach grime, blood, red wine—even shoe polish!—and discarded every which way. Once I found fish heads wrapped in the bath towels—guts, fins, scales. Someone had used the hotel linen for cleaning their catch! And not a tip among them.

It was out East. Fancy-smancy. I won't say where. The guests would come for the whales—tour boats and sightings during migration—and it was more often men with men and women with women than families or couples, if you know what I mean. And no disrespect, but two men in a king are seldom the neat freaks portrayed on TV.

This Hilton's better, here in Chicago, and not because it's where I grew up. I think it's being in the Midwest. That couple just seemed midwestern, as I said, though she was the friendlier one, like she had some job that required her to be friendly—as a receptionist or a hostess or something—but it wasn't enough to satisfy her, eight hours a day. More like friendliness was in her nature, and it spilled out naturally. The guy too, though he was more reserved than her, older.

To be honest, I hardly deserved the tips. They reused their towels, put trash in the baskets, rinsed the glasses . . . The most I ever had to do was change the bedding.

I left the day after they checked out. *Retiring*, I told Human Resources. I mean, I've got thirty-some years in altogether, and no reason to stay. There's Will's pension, Social Security in a few years, and Grace in California, living it up, no plans to provide me with grandkids. So I tell Francine—she's been with Hilton nearly as long as me—there's no reason not to.

It was the sheets that had done it. The grayish tinge in the middle, like a body'd laid there, unwashed, for a week. And those were the ones I put on clean. So I'm on my way down the hall to get another set, when the couple comes back for their coats—they decided to walk in Grant Park, cold as it was—and it's like they're embarrassed to interrupt. All apologetic. Their own room!

So I put on the other sheets, but the tinge is still there. A kind of shadowy impression, like you'd see on one of those shrouds at the Field. That's when I called Francine and we changed everything again—even the pads underneath—another set of linens and everything, but I could still see it, though Francine, when I asked her, wasn't really sure . . .

So I quit. Get out while the gettin's good, I always say. The tips were a sign. Such a cheerful couple! So generous!

Impaired

If it wasn't for the fact that I get turned on seeing Libby in her fancy clothes, I wouldn't have so readily agreed to attend her boss's affair. Left up to me, we would have RSVP'd *Sorry* and stayed home.

For one thing, occasions that require sports jackets and etiquette are not, as they say, my cup of tea. I'd rather order pizza from Dominos and veg out in sweats on the couch, even if that means watching one of Libby's lame chick-flick comedies, like *You've Got Mail* or *What's Up, Doc?* I mean, I don't really mind what we watch when we don't have to go out, because I want to please her, now that we're married. Not to mention that it never ceases to amaze me how horny a woman can get after watching those kinds of movies, even for the umpteenth time.

For another thing, I don't much care for Libby's boss, a supreme piece of corporate work, right down to her name: Harlequin Drummer—"Harly," for both the long and the short of it. "*Never* call her Harlequin," Libby huffed, the first time I'd repeated the name out loud. "Never *ever*. She's hyper about it."

Granted, before the specialty printed invitation arrived in

our mailbox, I'd only encountered Harly a couple of times—times when I'd stopped by North Bank Components to take Libby to lunch. I wasn't impressed. Something about the woman puts me off. She is too tall, for one thing, Amazonian tall, and she has a way of looking at people, even people my height—six-feet two—that makes them feel small. She has big hands and a firm handshake, an imposing voice. More than once, I'll bet, she's been mistaken as transgendered. Yet she is all woman otherwise—attractive in the way confident, unnaturally dark-haired women are, her eyes the sea green of Mediterranean travel brochures—glitteringly clear and enticing, likely deeper than they appear. Perhaps that's what initially turned me off about her, that incongruity, like one finds with those Alaskan sled dogs—the ones with powerful, wolf-like bodies but eyes like unworldly gems.

Or maybe it's because of how much Libby admires her. Not only because she's Libby's first female CEO—someone to emulate—but also because Harly took a liking to Libby early on, hiring her as first-shift supervisor even before the factory was completely up and running, which has allowed Libby in turn to handpick her own cadre of assemblers, although she has yet to actually finish her management degree, Personnel being one of the three courses she has left.

Still, in what I've come to think of as a domestic concession, I've had to accept the fact that I would at times be party to some uppity, North Bank Components get-together, seeing that I was, as the embossed invitation stipulated, Libby's "husband, partner, or significant other."

"Try to be charming," Libby repeated, as we jostled in front of the bedroom mirror on the evening of the big event. She had taken over the reknotting of my tie after my third or fourth attempt.

"Yes, dear," I replied. I modulated my voice in imitation of the proper husband, like one of the milquetoasts in *Father Knows*

Best or *Leave It to Beaver,* TV shows that have become my model for husbandry.

"And you *will* behave," she said, tapping my nose lightly with the nail of her index finger, a gesture that always drives my desire to ravish her on the spot. She no doubt orchestrated her perfume to swill my libido as well. *If you do that during the dinner,* I was about to say, *there'd be no guarantee.* But I could tell that she was in no mood for my kidding around, so I gave her the answer I knew she'd want to hear.

"Of course I'll behave," I said. "I'll be the gentleman you thought you married." And I kissed her reassuringly on the forehead.

We arrived at Harly's brick-skirted split-level a well-timed fifteen minutes after we were expected—my best guess at what would be acceptable tardiness in formal circumstances—only to find just two other cars in the circular drive, an Audi and a Jeep Grand Cherokee. I had hoped that we wouldn't be too early, and that, given the apparent grandeur of the affair, a crowd would already have formed. Not that I'm crazy about crowds either. It's more about social dynamics: The larger the group, the less one has to participate. Even in a small crowd, I can hunker down in a corner, behind a buffer of strangers, and leave the mingling to Libby. She loves to mingle, her very pores ooze friendliness. It's one of the things that attracted me to her.

But two cars could not have brought a crowd. "You're sure we're not too early?" I asked.

"We're not too early," Libby said. Something in the way she emphasized the words suggested that she wasn't completely sure herself.

"This is the right night, isn't it?" I said, slightly teasing.

"*Yes,*" Libby hissed.

Come to find out, the two couples who were there already would be the only other guests at the dinner party for which we'd received our gilded, embossed invitation. There were eight of us all together, counting Harly and her "other"—Ben, who was Harly's first and fourth husband.

"The first time was a disaster," she explained during cocktails, in a voice that, to me, sounded a little too well practiced. She was sitting on the left arm of the reddish overstuffed chair that Ben had sunk into shortly after we'd followed him across the slate entryway and into the living area. While it was clearly the most comfortable seat in the sand-colored room filled with predominantly iron and glass furniture, Ben had made no gesture to offer the seat to anyone else.

"The first time we were too young, too wild," Harly continued. "We had no idea what it meant to be married. By our three-month anniversary, we'd both sought diversions." Her tone hinted of nostalgia.

"We couldn't *not* fuck other people," Ben said, in such a deadpan tone that the profanity startled me. Except for his good-host greeting at the beveled glass door—*Come in, make yourselves at home*—he'd barely said a word up until then. Only settled into the overstuffed chair. Harly had done all the talking, the introductions. Now I'm no prude, but quite frankly, I never expected such language, given the semiformal atmosphere. But no one else seemed to take offense.

"No, we couldn't," Harly repeated with a short laugh. She flashed her green eyes at me, but the word *we* seemed to hang in the air like the scent of cheap candles.

Ben was a lawyer, it turned out, attached to the legal division of EKNOR Corporation, which owned North Bank Components. I didn't catch his last name, although I'm sure it wasn't Drummer. He was sixty-ish, slightly bald on top, but with neatly trimmed, mostly still black hair around his rather large ears. He seldom smiled, though his eyes did give off a certain glint that suggested he wasn't a total bore. There may have been, in fact, an attempt at humor in his cussing. He was slightly shorter than Harly, muscular and trim, as if he regularly worked out. Unlike the rest of us, who had dressed in ways that we assumed were appropriate for a dinner party, Mr. Harly—as Libby often refers to him around our house—wore chinos, slippers without socks, and a polo shirt open at the throat.

It was obvious from the introductions that Libby already knew one of the other couples, or at least Bill, the head of the shipping department at North Bank Components. His partner was Julie, who I'd later learn was in the process of a divorce from her first husband—which was not Bill. Julie and Bill had begun a "typical office affair" at the last place they'd both worked, and so, when he accepted the job here in North Bank, she'd followed.

The other couple—Gene and Jan—were friends of Harly's from one of *her* prior jobs, which included some time in Germany. The couple were maybe even native to Europe, for they were impossibly polite and each had a hint of some foreign accent, though I had no idea what it was. From what I understood, they had been friends of Harly's third husband, Henry, as well.

So it was awkward, at first. Nothing like what I'd hoped for. Harly, Libby, and Bill mostly talked shop, joking about employees at North Bank Components, only one or two names of which I'd heard Libby mention before. Julie had entered into some conversation with Gene and Jan. Ben had excused himself to do something concerning dinner. That left me just sitting quietly, *behaving*, trying not to undress Libby in my mind, and numbing my boredom with a pretty good single malt scotch, my second.

During a lull in conversation, Gene inquired as to what I did for a living. I had no sooner begun to explain how field officers of the Michigan Department of Natural Resources are not just "carcass jockeys"—Harly's phrase for those of us who at times must collect samples from the remains of car-deer encounters—that is, how we also study wildlife populations and maintain reforestations—when Ben's return prompted Harly to ask him if the grill was ready. His affirmation cut my monologue short. We were ushered out to the deck, where we were encouraged to fabricate our own kabobs by assembling on wooden skewers hunks of raw, marinated chicken, shrimp, pork, or beef. There were quartered onions, slices of green, red, and orange peppers, cherry tomatoes, artichoke hearts, broccoli and cauliflower (which we could eat "raw as a virgin," Harly clarified, or use to decorate our entrée), as well as assorted plates of cheeses, breads, and crackers, not to mention bowls of black and green olives, pickles, and other relish. We would be our own "grill masters," or, Harly quipped, if we needed help, Libby was the assembly supervisor—she'd be the one to consult.

It was surely not the kind of party I had anticipated—or dressed for—though, quite frankly, that suited me just fine. As it turned out, after some brief, overly-polite maneuvering around the buffet—a modest jockeying that was by no means limited to Libby and me—the combination of slippery, marinated meats and hungry, close-pressed bodies dissolved our communal fear of embarrassment and launched us like ravenous cicadas from our exoskeletal façades. The whole affair began developing into a surreal, intimate event, an entertainment of charred shrimp and raw beef, of flash-fired vegetables and marinade recipes. We began to relax, and it appeared that a good time would indeed be had by all.

The booze helped considerably, of course. I'll give Harly that much. She's no slouch when it comes to plying her guests with good liquor. We'd started with whatever we preferred from the corporately stocked wet bar—scotch, imported beer, mixed drinks—and then progressed through a number of wines and spirits as we buzzed like yellow jackets between the grill and the table lined with bowls of meat. First some champagne tinged with a kind of berry-flavored liqueur. Then some white wine— if we were having shrimp—some red, if we were separating our pepper slices with beef. (Both if we had skewered both.) Then some thick sweet port, and then brandy.

Darkness had enveloped us by the time we'd gotten to the

brandy, and I was exhausted. It had been *work* assembling the meal and devouring it. Not to mention the booze, and the fact that the skin on my face felt like I'd leaned too close to the grill a few times. I was stuffed and sleepy, and began drifting in and out of my surroundings. So I was not sure how long Julie had been talking to me when I was finally able to stir myself aware.

Right away, I noticed two things. Julie was babbling like a co-ed who had had one too many margaritas, flirty and loose. And she was attractive. Nothing like Libby and her businesslike body, her botanical-soaped freckles, her small, perfect breasts, her intense desire to manage. Nor did Julie have Harly's gargantuan glamour, her larger-than-life sexuality. Julie was countrified, simple, down-to-earth. Her long hair veiled the front of her strapless dress enticingly; to my booze-dulled imagination she was likely free-spirited and hard-nippled. I leaned in to listen.

She was telling me how lucky Libby was to find me, how her—Julie's—first marriage had been such a mistake, how her husband was making the divorce so difficult because he'd been embarrassed—after the fact—that so many other people at work had known what was going on with her and Bill, while her husband—he was management as well—didn't have a clue. He'd never questioned her about the extra hours she'd put in—they worked different shifts. No, he'd been more interested in his stupid NASCAR racing and the stupid Corvette he was restoring in the stupid pole barn. But a damaged ego makes divorce nasty, Julie said, and she hoped that it would never come to that with us. She *knew* it wouldn't, she said. She knew I was better than that. And she rested her hand on my arm as evidence of her certainty. Her touch sent a pulse to my crotch.

About then I heard Libby laugh. She was sitting at the other picnic table with Harly and Bill. Either Bill had said something funny or else Libby was laughing at his somewhat clumsy disengagement from the bench affixed to the picnic table.

"Are you okay to drive?" I heard Harly ask.

"No, *sir*," Bill replied. "But I'm sure Julie is—my designated driver."

When Julie smiled and stood up, two new revelations hit me. For one, Julie was not drunk. She hadn't been drinking anything but lemonade; her flirtation had simply been my sottish perspective. And for another, Gene and Jan were already gone; I could vaguely recall their nice-to-meet-yous interrupting Julie's talk.

Ben was just returning from inside the house with a fresh glass of brandy. He offered to show Bill and Julie to the door, but Bill insisted Julie could find the way. After they said their goodnights—and after another warm squeeze of my arm from Julie—I made my way to where Libby sat. I suggested that we should probably get going as well, that it was getting late.

But Libby pointed to her glass. "I'm not quite done," she said. She motioned for me to sit beside her.

Ben asked if I wanted anything else, and for a moment I considered the option. But then I also noticed how the tiki torches were swaying unnaturally and concluded that the dizzying buzz in my ears was likely more than tree frogs or crickets. I said, "I'd better not. I have to drive."

There was a kind of pregnant pause then, as the four of us sat at a picnic table scattered with various shaped wine and cocktail glasses, napkins, a bowl of mixed nuts (which I didn't recall seeing earlier), and one paper plate of different colored cheese cubes—as if someone had dumped all the separate leftovers onto a single pile. Libby and I faced Ben, who sat on the opposite bench. Harly was at the head of the table, slouched in a canvas director's chair. (*How appropriate*, I thought to myself, in a moment of clarity).

The night was pleasant—warm, starlit, and calm—and I began to wonder how they managed to keep the mosquitoes away. From the deck, I could see at the bottom of the yard a small lily pond, perfect for insect breeding, and yet I hadn't noticed any-one bothered by mosquitoes all evening.

"Wise decision," Harly said suddenly. It took me a moment before I realized the comment had to do with my refusing a last drink. Her voice drew our attention. It was obvious that she had something she wanted to say.

"What happened to me," she began, "happened after a company get-together in Munich, when I worked for the Visional subsidiary. Germans, you know, are big drinkers, like all Europeans. It's just expected—especially if you want to get along in business. Drinking's as much a part of the culture as driving is, if you think about it. With their reputation for high-speed automobiles—Mercedes, BMW, Volkswagen—it's always surprised me that there weren't more accidents. At any time of the day or night, probably half the people on the autobahn are inebriated . . . " The word *inebriated* caused her some problem, but we all knew what she'd meant.

She paused and looked hard at Ben, then at Libby and me. The greenness of her eyes was haunting. I began to wonder if Harlequin Drummer was expecting some kind of affirmation or response. But no one said anything.

"I was married to Henry, at the time," she said. "We'd gone to some shindig in Munich, some beer *garten* that Visional had rented in order to host the event, and we'd probably been among the last ones to leave. I was pretty fucked up, but not nearly as bad as Henry. So I drove.

"It was pretty late—or early, depending on how you look at it, probably four in the morning—and I remember having difficulty seeing, not only because I was blitzed, but because the fog was as thick as shit. I mean, you could literally cut it with a knife—a *cheese* knife—it was thick as white cheese. But at least I was on the right side of the road, at least we weren't in England or anywhere . . . "

She paused again, took a sip from her glass, hesitated, almost as though she expected Ben to take the story from there, as some couples do, as Libby has been known to do for me at times, even finishing a story that we were both familiar with, especially if I wasn't telling it the way she thought it should be told. But then I recalled that Ben had not been in Germany, as far as I knew. Harly was talking about a time before her remarriage to him.

She continued: "I was going faster than I should have in that fog, I'll admit. I mean, not like ninety or anything—I wasn't *that* out of it—but I was probably clipping along at fifty or so when suddenly we came upon a stalled car in my lane—at least I thought I was still in my lane, though it was difficult to tell—and I jerked the wheel hard"—she half-spun her clutched right hand and drink-filled left as a kind of demonstration, losing a swallow of brandy to the decking—"and barely made it by, the passenger side of my car collapsing and screeching as we hit the driver's side of the car that was stopped . . . The next thing I knew Henry was screaming and nearly in my lap, what with the glass from his window everywhere . . . " Something about that image made her laugh. "I managed to pull to the side of the road and stop, and we went back to see if anyone had been in the car."

She paused again. This time, I think, for effect.

"Well, it seems someone had. And not only that, but he'd had his arm out of the window when we hit—quite possibly waving us to go around. Henry and I found the man in shock. I'd apparently sheared off the better part of his left arm when our cars collided. We later found the arm in the road."

I heard Libby gasp at that point; myself, I was caught in a kind of stunned disbelief, numbed in large part by the mixture of alcohol I'd consumed. At the same time, given what I knew of Harlequin Drummer, I wondered if we were being played with on account of our drunkenness. Or if the story itself was meant to sober us up so that our trip home wouldn't be so disastrous.

"I know it sounds unbelievable," Harly said, as though reading my mind, "but it's the god-awful truth. And remarkably so-bering. Henry managed to pull himself together enough to apply a tourniquet with his belt. And the German lived. Last I heard, he had some kind of prosthetic arm . . . and with the generous insurance settlement, he's probably living better than he ever had before."

She took another drink. For a moment the only sound was crickets. It was as if no one knew what to say, though "no one" was likely just Libby and me, for I was sure that Ben was familiar with the story. He'd sat quietly throughout the narration, his right index finger circling the smooth lip of the brandy glass in front of him.

Finally, Libby asked, "What happened? Were you arrested or anything?"

Harly looked at her husband, number one and four. "That's where Ben reentered the picture," she said. "My knight in shining Armani. He was part of Visional's legal group in the States and was able to negotiate a settlement through the corporation's insurance. I was lucky. I pretty much walked away with only a bad memory—not that I recommend it."

"What happened to the arm?" I said, thinking that a little levity was in order.

Ben laughed. "It was brought into court as evidence," he said, "packed on ice in a beer cooler, like a trout."

"God!" Libby said, "That's gross!"

"Yes," he said. "It was . . . especially as it didn't help their case any."

Harly had grown quiet. It was just as well, because I'd heard all I wanted to. I feigned a yawn and asked Libby if she didn't think we should get going soon—now that I was sober enough to drive, thanks to Harly's story. Libby agreed. We said our good-byes. And as the night was clear and the traffic was light, we were soon safe at home.

"That was horrible," said Libby, when we'd settled into bed.

I had scooted into the middle and pulled her to me. She was not resistant, but less than enthusiastic. I was hoping that Harly's fateful little story hadn't put a kibosh on some after-party love-making, which I was suddenly in a very strong mood for. "Do you think it was true?" she asked.

"I suppose so," I said, nuzzling. "Why would she make up something like that?"

Libby lay quietly. She did not acknowledge my touch. She was clearly upset. It was obvious that I was not going to be counterseduced. I rolled onto my back, certain that she wanted to talk. She settled into the crook of my arm, the way well-practiced married people learn to, I suppose, sublimating desire to comfort, sex to companionship. Suddenly, I could see us fifty years from now lying on a bed not unlike this one, in the same embrace, thankful for the years that had been good to us, the years we'd had when sex was thrilling, and then the years when one or the other of us simply complied out of love. I could see us—it was definitely us—and yet, oddly, I was looking at us from a distance as well, looking down on us fifty years from now—and immediately I knew what Libby was going to say next. I knew what she was going to say and I prayed that she wouldn't say it. *Please don't*, I thought. I could feel her bare skin next to mine, her small perfect breast pushed against my chest. I could feel her perfectly smooth leg as it lay against the length of my own. I could feel her breathing on my neck, smell the toothpaste on her breath, and I knew what she was going to say.

"Would you still love me if I lost an arm?" she asked.

"Yes," I said quickly.

"Or a breast?"

"Yes, I'd still love you."

She rolled onto me then, skin upon skin, the full length, and I could tell by the moonlight that poured in through our open window that she was looking me straight in the eye, the way she did when she was deciphering my teasing for the truth. Then she tapped her fingernail against my nose. I stiffened at her touch.

"Would you still love me if I was impaired in some other way, if we couldn't have sex?"

"Yes, Libby," I said. "I'd still love you. I'll always love you. It's not just about sex."

"Liar," she said, without the hesitation I'd expected. And then she rolled off and turned her back to me and made sure there was the weight of a blanket between us.

I'd like to say I did the right thing then, that I reached over and tried to reassure her, to comfort her. But I didn't. I couldn't move. All I could think about was the arm in the road. I could picture it—a fish-pale, limp appendage gleaming in the halogen-lit fog. I could see it, the fingers twitching; and I could feel it as if it were my own arm reaching for something that was no longer there, something that would never be there again.

Within an Inch of the Burnished Knob

Within an inch of the burnished knob, the hand hesitates. An insignificant moment, a pause of the inevitable. And yet, in a pause, evitable and significant. Let us consider the circumstances. He has been gone twenty years, into the hills above the cemetery, or down the street to the tobacconist's for a cherry blend, his favorite. He has seen the fantasies of years to come, the small bowlers of weather, has rented a flat two streets over, grown a beard and, incognito, taken another wife. Did he wander off to some wild gaming mindlessly, or with perfect intent? The shirtsleeves and collar are frayed, faded to the milk-blue of an impatient dawn just before light. And just before light, in a fog-dampened, brick-red morning late in the millennium, his trousers—or shall we call them pants or, maybe, pantaloons—trail gray threads like curses, and he is drunk. Or has been drunk and now is sober, newly attired in stiff suede, a purple necktie tightened in a perfect Windsor near the throat, one fashion he's thankful to have snugged there, given the dichotomy of knots.

Within an inch of the burnished knob, the hand hesitates. The fingers short and stubby, in spite of his overall size, a healthy few inches over six feet, or more. To see his feet, however, we'd see a size eight or less, in tan, leather-thwacked oxfords, with the bold cuff of his pants bunching and wrinkled on the laces. Or athletic shoes, although they surely wouldn't have been so casual when he left. And consider the bush-luck of his extremities: Between the fingers there's little room for another's hand to spread as if in prayer; at his niece's wedding years before, congratulating the new father-in-law, one would have witnessed the handshake of a fish, fumbling and gone limp. Or firm and calloused, having mortared cement blocks for the better part of the years he's been gone, a job well below his schooling in foreign culture and language, but suitable for the deception. His fingers, long and elegant, have tentacled the tusks of many a piano, the small, quarter-moon cuticles gray with cement dust, or white and clean, scrubbed meticulously with pumice before he'd attempt to handle the crystal goblet of some pricey product of Gascony.

Within an inch of the burnished knob, the hand hesitates. And a slight breeze in the late afternoon tickles the fat finger hairs below the second knuckle, like a housefly, or when he drifts off to half-sleep in the heaviness of a summer's humidity, unable to keep at his briefs. He will flick at the light touch with the middle finger of his opposite hand, or he'll swat without looking, or he'll look and slowly swing the hand closer to his face to be certain before he swats at it. He will know that there is no fly, no insects but those in his imagination, the island free of evolution, nothing more than a nervous tick. Or he will not notice the wind at all, intent upon his mission, his familiar return or the initial movement of an unfamiliar door. The hand will move easily. And the hand will move away, or move to find the cold brass fingerprints that he had left there yesterday or the week before.

Within an inch of the burnished knob, the hand hesitates. Doubly, the moon reflects in the small triptych of windowpanes.

Doubly, he sees his face in the door, and the night has been long, and he longs to open the door and kiss his wife and cradle his daughter before she falls into dreams of princes at the window. A clown lamp, lit with balloons, giggles lightly near her bed. Or she sleeps on some mouse-soiled mattress on the uncarpeted floor, where he left her no visible means, and she awaits his mean deviation, confused by the warm wetness of her sex and the cramped brittleness of her submission. *Spoony tragediennes, their dreams are the same.* Or the hand is palsied, and he will reach in his trousers for a key, shaking, knowing that the door has been locked twenty years, or since morning. Is anyone home? His wife, hysterical, has died. She would dub her uterine cancer uxoricide. Years before he left, years after he left. He may enter and sort what memories may linger, or the hand may sign the paper that felled whole suburban blocks of single-family properties, sparing not a single lawnmower, not a single lava-stone of gas-fired grills.

Within an inch of the burnished knob, the hand hesitates. It has come to this: the barely visible scar where the ring once hooked the fencepost or where the lemonade can lid slit through the pointer. Where the stitches pulled and revealed the wrist muscle after the storm door shattered at his weight. Or where the palm of his blackened hand slapped the face of his mother, loud with concern for his alcoholic health, the big palooka. Or where his fingers once explored the wet cunt of a high school majorette. And there's the joke, now, not to eat with these, "you never know where they've been." *Oh where's the history of the hand, the palm we find in the reflection of the moon, doubly, the moon the size of a doorknob?*

Within an inch of the burnished knob, the hand hesitates. An inch of newspapers that he never read. Or that he read but didn't discard, or that he discarded after he clipped the coupons for cereals he knew would be too good to taste but not good for him, or good for him but not too good to eat. A yellowed inch of the wristwatch face, the timepiece passed on by his father twenty years before. It's his father's house, and he's returning, finally, to face the music. The piano lessons he quit when he left. Or it's the nursing home where the father lies in wait, befuddled and senile, hard of seeing. An inch of wood dust from the house he had rebuilt. An inch of pine board upon which his books rest, unread, and he is coming to pack them while she's not home so he doesn't have to see her face. Or an inch of pizza crust that she couldn't believe he wouldn't eat. Four times the depth of the zucchini seeds they planted the first year of their marriage. Twice the chill of a soaking October rain.

Within an inch of the burnished knob, the hand hesitates. As if sensing nitrostarch beyond the wood-core steel panel. As if unsure of the address, or of the moment, twenty years after the date was first made. Without backup. Solo. Heroics left to sorry adolescence. Shall he pause forever, or has she watched him coming up the walk, or slamming his jalopy in the drive, and knows she knows he's there and, if so, what good will the pause do? Behind the door guns are leveled, loaded with buckshot, more to wound than to kill. But he's dead already, nearly so, and hesitates to find the words for when the door will open. If at all. He wants to. He wants to reach and turn the knob and face the unknown, or he wants to turn away, it's no good, it's too late, nothing else can be done. So who hesitates? His heart has twitched, he can't fully breathe in, clears his ears, gasps. Hesitation is all he's capable of. Or he's not capable of hesitation. And he hasn't hesitated at all, only his hand has hesitated when the groceries slipped as he was about to.

Within an inch of the burnished knob, the hand hesitates. The hand of the salesman on the other side of the door, slipping away, having duped the wife into a lengthy sales pitch and quick fuck on the carpet, professionally vacuumed. His wife who, we can be sure, is easily duped. He's done it at times himself. Or he's not capable of duping her, nor she him. And she's turned them away, sent the salesmen packing dozens of times, sent him packing, and each time he returns, and reaches for the door, and hesitates, and in hesitating the world as he knows it, *the world as he knows it,* explodes. He is shrapnel; he is the gelatin of boiled chicken; he is the sweat of the basement floor when the summer stinks of humidity; he is the doll without clothes, whose loose eye thumps in the electric dryer like tennis shoes; he is the bones of infertile eggs; he is the voice of snow; he is the fat cock of possibility, the feral grant that grants him the right to hesitate. He is the hand hesitating, and all within an inch, more or less.

Within an inch of the burnished knob, the hand hesitates, considers, reconsiders, and drops, dumbly, to his pocket. He fingers the keys to his Oldsmobile. He turns, and without looking back, wades deep into the night over his head.

The Good Life

The year we sold the farm, Hank bought a boat. He called it "trading the garden for the good life."

It began the year before, the morning he came in for breakfast and complained that he was having trouble hitching the sprayer to the tractor. "Gettin' too old for this," he said, slumping into the dinette chair closest to the door. He claimed to be losing strength in his arms, and half-humorously attributed it to age. He looked pale, even more so than usual above his hat line. When he lingered over his coffee, I called the doctor from the bedroom phone—so Hank couldn't stop me—and scheduled him an appointment for a check-up.

After his bypass, Hank began to talk more often about retiring, about selling the orchards. After all, he reminded me, he'd been farming for the better part of forty years. "It's about time I started doing something else," he said.

"About time," I agreed, as I always did.

But I had heard such talk before. Every farmer I know imagines life without weather. Whenever there's too much rain or not enough rain, too much sun or not enough sun, whenever prices go up too high or down too low for too many years in a row—farmers talk about selling. "Selling out," they call it at the grange. For the better part of forty years, I'd heard Hank threaten to get rid of the "whole stinking mess" more times than I could count.

I guess I never thought he really meant it, not even the afternoon I found him and Drew—our son—hunched over the vacation maps and brochures that were piled on the kitchen table like implement catalogs. They didn't even look up when the screen *clacked* behind me.

"Ginny, you gotta see this," was all Hank said.

I remember setting the bags of groceries on the counter next to the refrigerator, thinking that the milk should be put away soon, before I went over to take a look. The table was thick with advertisements, though not what I'd expected, no shiny blue tractors or the latest sprayer designs. Instead, the leaflets pictured southern mansions and pecan-lined streets and harbors thick with sailing yachts strung as though for a holiday with flags of various colors and designs. Quaint boulevards framed horse-drawn carriages; Spanish moss dripped from cypress trees. One picture showed an alligator in a water hole at a golf course. And there were dozens of blue and green maps.

"Charts," said Drew, when I asked what the maps were of. "Maps are for land; charts are for water."

"Charts of what?"

"The Intracoastal Waterway," said Hank. "D'you know it's possible to get from Maryland to Florida in a boat and never actually go out into the ocean?"

"Why would I want to?" I said.

"We'd go south for the winter, and come back for summer," Hank said. "Live on a boat."

"And the farm?"

"Sell it. Do some traveling. You always complain that the farm keeps us from traveling. Now's our chance."

"But you've never been on a boat like that. Won't it be expensive?"

"You get a *sail*boat, Mom," said Drew. "Wind costs nothing. It'd be great. I'd even come see you during holidays."

Hank's gray eyes caught mine and held them. "You'd like to see the ocean, wouldn't you?" he said. I was chilled by the thought.

Still, in spite of my spending the better part of that afternoon browsing through promotions from every city and state along the eastern seaboard—and imagining what a different and exotic life that would be—I never actually believed Hank would go through with it. There had been so many other plans that had never come to pass.

The very next day, in fact, the tractor quit. We had it trucked to Buckley for repairs and Hank leased a dual-wheel John Deere from Cherryland Implements in order to get the seedlings disked. He cursed most of that week. The John Deere was more difficult to maneuver than our Ford, Hank said, and blamed the wheelbase. Then the weather turned rotten, and he couldn't disk at all, and Cherryland wouldn't discount the lease for downtime. For the next few weeks, Hank was so intent on simply getting things done that he'd not had time to think about what he had come to call "the good life."

Then, one day in June, I came in from weeding the flowerbeds and found Hank lying on the couch. I knew right away that something was wrong. While farming had always given Hank's face a ruddy, youthful flush, and his hat hid most of the gray that had just begun to invade his still enviably dark hair, on the couch Hank looked old. He was sweating, and his voice shook. His gestures were unsteady. His lips were gray. I covered him with the afghan and placed a nitro pill beneath his tongue; I called the hospital. Hank went in the ambulance without a struggle.

"A small stroke," said Dr. Achubi. "He's lost part of the feeling in his toes. We'll have to watch him for a few days and hope that the nerves regenerate. Otherwise—"

"You mean he can't walk?" I said, trying to get through the bedside manner and to the point.

"Oh, no, nothing like that. He may lose a toe or two. If the tissue begins to die, we'll have to remove it. But that's a worst-case scenario. We'll know in a few days. A couple weeks on crutches, maybe, some therapy, and he'll be right back at it, good as new. Nothing to worry about there."

The doctor's voice emphasized *there* in a way that suggested something was not being said.

"But?" I asked.

"But there's no telling how long his heart will hold up. Has he ever thought of retiring, of doing something a little less physical than farming?"

"Sailing," said Hank suddenly, in a raspy voice. Apparently he'd not been asleep, as the doctor and I had assumed as we talked across his bed.

"Ah, good," said Achubi. "But not until you're stronger, young man." He ordered another IV.

In the end, Hank lost three toes. But he was fitted with a special shoe, and in a few months, except for a slight limp, most people would never have known that one foot was a grotesque stump. He was back on the tractor in no time—against my better judgment, and in spite of Dr. Achubi's orders.

He wasn't "good as new." Hank tired more easily and often complained that his foot ached—especially when it rained or was cold. Winter was hard on him. He must have given a lot of thought that winter to what else he could be doing as he soaked his foot in Epsom salts, because that spring, when the developers came out with their annual offer to buy the orchards and develop a subdivision of single family homes—Paradise Hill Estates— Hank listened carefully. Then he sold.

"Enough to live on comfortably for the rest of our lives," he said, to convince me. "Cherries were getting too iffy."

We kept the house and the barns and about an acre for my vegetables and flowers. The real estate people liked the idea that the young couples buying these upscale houses could look out over vestiges of rural life and see the bay in the distance. They called it "the view."

Hank went to work part-time at Drew's frozen yogurt franchise, keeping books and occasionally—during the parades and such times—serving up tastes of Low-Fat Chocolate Cheesecake or Banana-Pineapple Split. Still, the closest we got to "the good life" that summer was Hank's birthday, when Drew gave him subscriptions to *Yachting* and *Travel and Leisure,* and they began to talk sailing.

By the end of August, on the hill above the house, where the cherries had been harvested in July, the orchards had all been bulldozed, and new roads and basements had begun to take shape. As the summer wore down, Hank began to spend more time watching TV, mostly *Cousteau* or *National Geographic.* He seemed to have lost interest in everything else. Or maybe I was too busy to notice. Unable just to sit and fuse to the recliner, I began to involve myself more actively in the church, the hospital auxiliary, the women's club at the grange. Hank ignored my entreaties to come along or to find himself something to do, so I kept busy to keep from worrying.

Drew tried, at least. He encouraged Hank to help out at the shop when he could. But with the summer season over, the yogurt crowds had thinned to regulars, and there was no real need of an additional person.

Then, in September, after one of my shifts at the hospital, I again found Hank sitting at the kitchen table, where all the charts and brochures that I thought had long been discarded were again spread out before him. He must have stashed them away somewhere, just waiting for the opportunity to drag them out and continue his planning.

"What would you say to a dream come true?" he asked me,

fingering a postcard-sized photograph that I hadn't remembered seeing before. I noticed that there were a number of new pictures and charts—several of the same boat, even what looked like an owner's manual, with dimensions and specifications spelled out. It was the boat in the photograph he held, a bright red single-masted sailboat. A *sloop*, I'd learn later. Suddenly I was suspicious, and the cold chill came back. Hank was grinning like a child with a new toy.

"You didn't go out and buy a new boat, did you?" I said. My voice was a giveaway. Any excitement I may have wanted to express was tempered by concern. I'd never actually been on a boat that size, nothing larger than an aluminum fishing boat— not counting the ferry we had taken across Lake Michigan when Drew was ten.

"No, I didn't buy a *new* boat," he said, somewhat elfishly.

"You bought a *used* boat?" I asked.

"Not exactly."

"Then what, Hank?"

"Remember that thirty-seven acres near Escanaba that Uncle Walter willed to me? I traded it—for *this*." He held up the photograph of the red-hulled boat.

"Traded it?"

"Even Steven. The guy wants to build up north and retire. He owns a tool and die in Chicago. Used the boat as a vacation home."

"In Chicago?"

"In Leland."

"But—"

"Oh God, Ginny, she's *beautiful!*"

I had forgotten all about the property in the Upper Peninsula. Suddenly I recalled that the reason we had taken the ferry across Lake Michigan in the first place had been to settle Uncle Walter's estate and to look at the property; we had driven up from Menominee to Escanaba, and then come back over the Mackinac Bridge. It had been one of the few vacations we had taken. It seemed ironic now that all these events were somehow related.

I was apprehensive, to say the least. Not that I was afraid of the boat itself; after all, I was a passable swimmer—we had had an aboveground pool when Drew was young—but I was concerned that we were getting into something we knew nothing about. And I wasn't sure Hank could handle it.

Hank, on the other hand, was undaunted by the unknown. For the first time in years he was visibly excited, and his enthusiasm began to fuel mine.

"It needs a little work, of course. It's not new. But the guy at the dry dock says I can get in during the winter and clean her up."

"Dry dock?"

"That's what they call it when they take the boats out of the water for winter. Drew and I will spruce her up during the winter and then we'll put her in the water in the spring."

"But you don't know anything about sailing," I said.

"Neither did John Winston when he first bought it. He said the Coast Guard offers courses on navigation and stuff during the winter. We'll just have to find out where. After a summer of practice—and if *you* like it, of course—we can head south next fall."

"We'll see about *that*," was all I could think to say. And so we did. We drove out to Leland that very afternoon.

The boat was beautiful, I guess, though it did appear to be weathered. The sails were a creamy yellow color and had a few tattered edges. The wood was faded gray, like driftwood, and the varnish flaked off at the touch. But the fiberglass seemed intact; there didn't appear to be cracks anywhere in the hull. A little encouragement from the marina mechanic got the four-cylinder started in short order.

"Could use new plugs," said Hank.

I had begun to calculate just how much work was involved

when I noticed that Hank, for the moment at least, had lost his limp. He was cheerful and interested. I wondered if this boat might be what he needed to get his mind off the TV or his bird feeders, and I couldn't help but feel good for him. Maybe it was about time our lives took a new direction—a new *tack*, as Hank would soon be saying.

"What's it called," I asked the man at the dock.

"A Catalina 30," he said.

"But what's its name? Don't these boats have names?"

"Wind's Town," said Hank. "After John's last name. Winston—Winds Town. But we'll call it something else, I guess."

"Definitely something else," I said, and I began to consider the possibilities.

We documented her with the Coast Guard as the *LeeSure Lady*. The man who did the lettering on the stern suggested the pun, since she was a sailboat. Hank was thrilled. "Why hadn't *I* thought of that," he said.

He spent all winter working on her. He sanded and varnished the wood, patched the fiberglass, polished the brass, painted and scrubbed. There wasn't a spot on the boat that didn't get Hank's attention. He even sent one of the sails to a sailmaker in California to be resown.

I'd go over on the weekends and watch. At first, I offered to help, but after Hank took classes two nights a week at the Maritime Academy, he became a little obsessive about how things were supposed to be done.

"Do you want this rope wound up like the others?" I'd ask.

"*Line*," he'd say.

"What?"

"It's a line when it's attached to a boat."

"Then do you want the line wound up?"

"*Coiled*, you mean. No, I'd better do it."

While at times I felt the boat was becoming competition for me, taking the place of a mistress—after all, Hank called the boat *she* and *her*, and treated her with special care, going even so far as to buy her little gifts, like new hardware or "lines"—I also began to understand how some women who know that their husbands are having affairs continue to keep it secret. Hank was buoyant around the *LeeSure Lady*; for the first time in years he seemed to be enjoying his work. He stopped complaining about his foot, and I barely noticed his limp. On deck of *LeeSure Lady*, he was as agile as a member of a well-trained racing crew. He seemed to be carried away by visions of bearing a course for the Gulf Stream somewhere between Long Island and Bermuda, sunny skies and a steady breeze, porpoises playing off the bow.

His happiness was enough for me.

On April 15, Tax Day, we had the *LeeSure Lady* lifted into the water. We were fortunate to have dockage; John Winston had "willed" us his slip at the marina. When Hank wouldn't let me break a bottle of champagne across the *Lady*'s bow, we opened it and drank it out of paper cups. Hank had done a wonderful job with the boat. Even on that cold, gray April afternoon, the *LeeSure Lady* burned warm and red against the dull pilings.

Not unlike farming, sailing depends a lot on the weather, and as our luck would have it, the weather turned ugly the day after we secured the boat in our slip, and it stayed nasty right through Memorial Day. As May passed, Hank became more and more despondent. There was nothing he could do but recoil a few lines or swab the seagull droppings off the deck. He had been so looking forward to his first sail that the extended foul weather nearly drowned him in depression.

That was when Drew and I decided something had to be done.

On Memorial Day, despite a slight rain and forty-eight degrees, Drew and his new girlfriend, Trudy, met us at the boat for a picnic. The men rigged the sails, which we had gotten back weeks before. Then they raised the ensign—Drew's boat-warming present—a small flag with a martini glass on it. But I served hot coffee instead of cocktails, and we ate our picnic below deck. Hank talked with muted animation about jibs and constellations, as we plotted warm harbors for Thanksgiving.

That evening, for the first time in weeks, Hank complained that his foot ached, so I drove home.

We finally got good weather on June seventh. We loaded the *LeeSure Lady* with enough canned food and water for a few days, Hank's fishing tackle, our life vests and clothes, cooler, Sterno, matches, and whatever else we could think of. We intended only to sail for the day, but Hank said, "You never know for sure." He thought that if we couldn't find our way back for some reason, we'd at least be prepared.

But the engine wouldn't start. It seems that the radio had been left on when we were there on Memorial Day, and the battery was dead. By the time the marina workers jump-started us, it was already afternoon.

"We don't need to hurry," Hank said, halfheartedly. "We have everything we need on board."

"Everything," I agreed. But I could see the anguish in his eyes.

We motored slowly out into the harbor and around a few times to get used to the way the *LeeSure Lady* responded. Hank had me at the helm. Then Hank checked the direction of the wind and turned us in the proper tack so that we could sail directly out beyond the break wall once the sails were hoisted. "Keep her steady," he yelled as he worked his way toward the mast.

I watched Hank untether the halyard and wind it around the winch. He inserted the crank handle.

"Ready?" he shouted.

"Ready!" I replied. And I was. *Finally.* I looked off to the right side the starboard to see how far we were from the rocks. I wanted to be sure that I was keeping the boat steady.

When I looked back, Hank was half-lying on the cabin deck

with one arm caught in the rope near the winch. His eyes were closed tight; his lips were pursed so hard that I thought for sure he couldn't breathe. I shut off the engine and scrambled to him. The sail, raised about six or seven feet, luffed and flapped and clanged against the mast. When I finally got to Hank, he was completely covered by the bulk of the canvas that hadn't yet been raised. He was alive, but unconscious. As I freed his arm from the winch, I began to scream for help.

How I ever thought to turn off the engine, I'll never know. I don't remember Hank ever explaining to me how to operate it. Still, I have somehow always been able to keep my wits in emergencies. Maybe I had subconsciously learned about the boat by watching Hank so often; maybe I had wondered at some time what I would do if something like this happened, and I remembered it in order to be prepared. I don't know. The boys from the marina who heard me yelling and who rowed out and took Hank back to the dock, where the ambulance met us, said that my shutting off the engine probably saved the *LeeSure Lady*. But for some reason, I wasn't very comforted by that thought.

They took Hank directly to Munson Medical Center in Traverse. I rode in the back with him. And it was during that ride in the ambulance that I noticed how thin his face had gotten. He had seldom removed his gold-braided captain's cap, which Drew had given him when he first bought the boat. Traded for his farm hat. But bareheaded and drained of color, the Hank in the ambulance was more like a poor wax model of himself. A death mask. He looked so unnatural that I finally placed the cap—I was carrying it for some reason—back on his head. I took his hand in mine.

"He's had a good one," Dr. Achubi said, when we finally arrived.

Hank now lies in a hospital bed, tethered to life by three machines. One breathes for him; one pumps his heart; one monitors his brain. I can't look at them any longer. The green lines on the monitor remind me of the waves that were splashing against the break wall at Leland as the *LeeSure Lady* bumped against the rocks, scraping the red paint that Hank had so carefully applied in perfect coats during the winter.

To this day, I'm not sure who rescued her, who returned her to the slip and tied her there. But I continue to assure Hank that she's okay and that she's waiting for him. I tell him that the lines are coiled properly, that it's warm in the inland waterway, and that I'd like to be in Jacksonville for Christmas.

I don't tell him that it's April again—Tax Day—and that he's been comatose for ten months. I don't tell him that I've sold the *LeeSure Lady* to pay his medical bills. And I don't tell him that I have to decide in a few weeks whether or not to have these damn machines shut off.

Instead, I wait. Like a sailor's wife. I keep busy as a volunteer at the hospital, so I can look in on him, and I imagine in my faithful heart that someday he will return. I imagine he's just off the coast of somewhere—living the good life—and on a healthy tack toward home.

Empty Nest

Ellen kept two feeders on the deck—the clumsy wooden one Harry Jr. had made in eighth-grade shop class, many years before, and the newer, red plastic, barn-shaped one she'd bought on sale at Walmart. Three others were spaced in the yard: one in the shape of a gumball machine on a pole near the back fence, and two smaller tubes in the crab apple that, when filled, weighed the branches nearly to the ground.

At times it was a challenge to keep the feeders filled. Gray squirrels, scavenging for oiled sunflower seeds, scattered discards in every direction; the jays made noisome pigs of themselves. Still, Ellen didn't mind. *Better to feed than to be fed upon*, she always said. She'd take her coffee to the reading chair near the patio door and chart their comings and goings.

The birds gave her days purpose, and she marked them accordingly. When Harry Jr. phoned about his promotion, Ellen celebrated by loading the feeders with Premium Songbird Mix. On the anniversary of Harry Sr.'s fatal accident, she poured twenty pounds of corn beneath the cedars in the side yard, where five turkeys had appeared the day before.

"Aren't you becoming a little obsessive," Harry Jr. said, the next time he called. "For the record, I'm concerned."

Ellen had been telling him about the crows. They had arrived in a scuffle of snow, and the contrast—black against white—was brutal. Even the jays seemed intimidated.

"They are more like people than you can imagine," she said.

"It's an expense you don't need," Harry Jr. replied. "You should cut back."

She laughed girlishly at the thought: *Maybe woodpecker suet for Valentine's, hummingbird nectar for her birthday, maybe grape jelly for the orioles . . .*

"They carry disease," her son continued, "and they make a mess of the yard."

"How's Carol?" she asked, to change the subject. "How are the boys?"

"They take care of themselves," Harry Jr. said. "They'll survive without you."

It was a moment before Ellen realized he was still talking about the birds. And while it may have been true, it was also nothing she didn't know already. Days after she'd thought they had gone, she'd found the body of one crow near the fence, dark holes where the eyes should have been.

The Last Swim of the Season

The gold-speckled Formica was now gray countertop. Stainless steel had replaced the hideous green enamel sink (dulled by a young girl's angry scrubbing with a Brillo pad), and someone had painted the lower cabinets a dark red—surely the tenth or eleventh coat of cheery color on doors that never latched completely to begin with. Beyond that, the kitchen area was much the same as the last time she'd been there, with Dan: stacked randomly on the open shelves above the counter were mismatched dishes and cups, more than a few of which were the knockoff Delft pattern she'd recognized as once belonging to her grandmother's summer place—typical housewares of a Michigan cottage. The plumbing hadn't been updated either, if the musty, mineral-rich, lead pipe and ant-powder smell of the place was any indication. But except for the countertop and sink, and a few recent photos of her sister Susan's family anchored by Home Depot magnets on the fridge, the only recognizable difference in the kitchen was a Post-it note on the outside of the cupboard to the left of the sink, where the coffee mugs were kept. It read: WHAT'S THE POINT?

"Dad?" she said.

The fact that the back door had been unlocked—as surely the porch door was—told nothing, for it was a rare occasion that her father would ever set the deadbolt, and then only if he could locate the key. It was, after all, an island, as he often reminded his daughters, a small island. Everyone knew everyone else, and they didn't reckon a thief among them. The removal of anyone's property—by tourists, say—would likely arouse the suspicion of the ferrymen, who were islanders. And besides, what was there to steal?

Standing now at the stainless sink and facing into the cabin-like space that realtors liked to promote as an "open floor plan," Karen could see the logic of her father's argument. Beyond the countertop "bar," which served as both an all-purpose table and a half-wall that separated the kitchen area from the living room, the familiar brown-and-red plaid sofa bed slumped like discarded laundry against the pine panels of the one windowless wall. Opposite was the fireplace, framed by windows. On the far wall, matching replacement windows were framed by bookcases stuffed with disorderly books, supine and perpendicular. The only other furnishings in the main room consisted of two aluminum folding chairs, a thick birch-legged coffee table, a small, pressboard entertainment center, and a folding card table, upon which paperwork crowded a laptop computer.

Karen shook her head. With the exception of the computer, there was little that anyone would likely want to steal.

"Dad? It's Karen," she said. Then louder: "Dad!"

The bathroom door was open; empty. Nor was he in the bedroom, always oddly spartan and neat, compared to the bookshelves, a quilted coverlet straightened on the double bed, photographs of Karen and her sister as young girls arranged carefully on the knotty pine dresser. Nor on the porch—the room that Karen, as an irritable adolescent, had occupied most often. Through the three walls of screened windows she could see up and down the shoreline in both directions, out onto Lake Michigan. But there was no sign of him walking the beach. And it was unlikely, given the temperature of the water, that he'd be swimming.

Still, there was evidence that he'd not been gone long: an unwashed coffee cup and cereal bowl in the sink, the reading lamp glowing beside the computer, a currently dated quart of milk in the fridge.

No smell of gas, Karen thought to herself. *No sign of foul play.*

If he'd gone to the store, he'd be back soon enough. After all, he'd not been told she was coming. There was no reason for him to hang around. Karen decided to brew a pot of coffee and wait on the porch. *Patience,* he'd often told her, *is no more than accepting the present moment on its own terms.*

"Have him tell his First Lady story," Susan had advised. "Or ask him about his column, his new book. Get him to talk about *anything.* Ask him why he's not answering my phone messages or e-mails. Be sure he's all right."

"I'm sure he's all right," Karen said. It was the third call she'd gotten from her sister in a week. By Susan's reckoning, their father had been kidnapped by some radical religious sect and forced into a vow of silence. Or else he'd drowned. Or been overcome by leaking fumes from the propane furnace. Susan hadn't heard from him in weeks; no one had heard from him in weeks. Even his editor had called Susan to ask if Dad was okay.

Karen was less than convinced. She offered reassurance. "It's not like it's the first time he's done this," she said.

Her sister sighed audibly, familiar histrionics. "Wasn't there a good reason before?" she said. "Wasn't it after mom's death? Wasn't it only a few days?"

"If something was wrong," Karen argued, "I'm sure we'd have heard. Maybe he's just got a new girlfriend . . ."

"Or maybe he's collapsed at his computer," Susan snapped.

"Come on, what's the likelihood of him having a relationship on an island of two hundred people!"

"I think there's more like four or five hundred, year-round—"

"So you're saying," the elder sister interrupted, in a voice Karen imagined someone might use to call 911, "is that you're *not* going to check up on him? That his *favorite* daughter is refusing to make a small effort and see if her father is okay? You can be sure that if *I* lived closer . . . "

Big IF, thought Karen. Yet there she stood again, side-by-side with Susan on the cliff of filial guilt, and her choices were limited: leap off in some calculated and prepared way—like strapped to a hang glider or parasail—or else risk Susan's spring-armed push, launching Karen, wingless, into some frothy emotional backwash. This time she was prepared.

"I guess I could go over this weekend and see what he's up to," she said finally, not letting on to Susan that she'd already made plans to do so.

"Good," Susan said. "Call me as soon as you know anything."

The First Lady story was one of three stories their father ever told, mostly at social occasions, and mostly to his daughters' embarrassment. He recounted in some detail the times he'd slept with the governor's wife. "She was really something," he'd begin. "Nothing against my girls' mother, of course, who in her day was competent enough . . . But Marly was *wild*, a real adventurer."

Karen would leave the room, if she could, furious that he could be so insensitive to other people's privacy—the governor's, their dead mother's—especially considering how hard he worked to protect his own. It was difficult for her to excuse his indiscretions, even after she'd come to believe that the stories were just his way of dealing with a depthless social insecurity, a chronic shyness. They seemed to come to him too naturally. He didn't need to be plied with alcohol to assume the role of a loose-lipped braggadocio; he merely had to be pressed into corners of small talk.

He'd tell the same stories over and again. Yet not completely. He'd never mention, for instance, that the woman he was claiming to have slept with had not been the First Lady at the time—that their trysts had taken place many years before, when the two of them were undergraduates at the same small college, and that it had been a time when many people were adventurers, when open sexuality was hardly a political risk, barely even shocking, even for a long-haired, sandal-footed, bead-laden girl from Boyle County, Kentucky.

To Karen, such incompleteness in his storytelling—what he implied by the omissions—made it close enough to a lie that she discounted the whole affair, particularly given the certain knowledge of who her father had actually become since his college days, during his more than twenty-year marriage to her mother, and then after her mother's cancer and death, when her father so isolated himself with his writing and books that he made a trip to the grocery store sound more like an obligation to attend some black tie event than a need for orange juice, coffee, or bread.

But what bothered Karen most about his stories was that the other people in attendance—his audience—wouldn't know the rest of the story, wouldn't have the certain knowledge she had, and that her father would reflect badly on her.

Just a couple months before, for the surprise birthday party Jules had orchestrated, Karen's father had taken the ferry to the mainland in order to attend. And he'd performed predictably. Pressed for conversation, he'd regaled a group of Karen's co-workers with his stories.

"Did your father really fuck the governor's wife?" Jules asked, after everyone had gone. Karen was stretching Saran Wrap across the leftover cake.

"*No*," she had answered, perhaps with more vehemence than she'd intended. "Not exactly. It's not the whole story." She explained how he left things out, how he'd exaggerated the sexuality for effect. And though she was more than a little disappointed in him, her fury had abated over the years, and she was able to control her anger in front of Jules. They'd not been lovers for long. They were still mapping a way through the geographies of prior relationships and personal incongruities. Karen didn't want her father's fabling to be an issue. She didn't want Jules to be disappointed in her because of her father.

"But it's a great story the way he tells it," Jules said. "You really shouldn't spoil it with the facts."

Jules had found her father charming. And that unsettled Karen even more.

She phoned him days later, her voice pitched and trembling. "Why can't you just—for once—tell *the truth*!"

He'd likely have been sitting where she was now, in the off-green wicker chair on the screened porch of the cottage, watching the slow progress of an ore freighter as it navigated the channel between Beaver Island and Charlevoix. His face would be absent of expression, sculptural, at most a reflection of melancholy, though no one would have been there to see the sad gray fringe encircling the blue intensity of his eyes. Karen always saw it, of course, even when he claimed everything was "peachy." When she looked closely into his eyes, she was reminded of all the sleepy, rainy, numb summer afternoons she'd spent on that same porch, bored and lonely.

Her blowup caused a long silence on the phone, as Karen knew it would. At the same time, she knew that if she stayed on the line long enough—and she liked to imagine that it *was* still a line, and not merely two voices carried on cellular frequencies—his silence would have been broken only after an interminable pause. "I don't really know how to respond to that," he'd have said, his single answer for everything that he didn't want to address.

But she hadn't waited. She'd quickly apologized for raising her voice and then changed the subject, as usual.

It had been the last time they'd spoken.

An anxious chirping startled her. At first, she determined to let her messaging service redirect the call, since it could only be someone wanting information she didn't have. *He's just not here*, she thought. But when the chirping began again, more insistently, Karen returned to the kitchen, where her phone thrummed beside the sink.

"*And?*" Susan said, before Karen had the phone completely to her ear.

"And he's not here," she said.

"Then where is he?"

"Susan, if I knew that, I could have saved myself a trip—and you some worry. He's probably just gone for a walk. There's evidence that he *was* here this morning . . ."

"Where are you?"

"At the cottage, of course."

"But he's not there?"

"*Susan.*" Karen modulated her voice to sound exasperated, something her anxious sister would surely be able to sense. "I haven't seen him yet, but a coffee cup and cereal bowl are in the sink. And I've only been here a short time . . ."

"So what are you going to do?" By the tone of her voice, Karen could tell that Susan was really asking if Karen was going to do what Susan wanted her to. As if Karen had no choice in the matter.

"I'll just wait for him, I guess. What else *is* there to do? The next ferry back isn't until tomorrow. If he doesn't appear by then, I'll report his absence to the constable."

"His *absence?* You sound like a goddamn schoolteacher. Aren't you even a little concerned?"

"I'm *here*, aren't I? Isn't that concern enough?" Leave it to an elder sister to raise one's hackles. The calm that had begun to envelop her on the porch was suddenly threatened by the dark clouds of Susan's manipulative anxieties. Tactics Karen was familiar with. "If you'll recall, Susan," she retorted, "I WAS a goddamn schoolteacher—for five goddamn years."

The line went silent, as if Susan had wandered out of service or the battery was low. It was the kind of silence Karen had grown accustomed to, working the phones at PDI. Not like a lost signal. There was enough faint static for Karen to imagine her sister rolling her eyes toward the ceiling of her bathroom, as she deftly changed one daughter's diaper with her free hand. Then a deep breath—Susan's way of getting back in control.

"I'm sorry, Kare-Bear," she said. "It's just one of those days, you know. Brian's at some kind of game thing with his office, and Jill's got diarrhea again. You *will* call me as soon as you find out something for sure?"

"Of course."

Closing the phone, she noticed that Jules had called at some point. But she wasn't in any mood to talk now, particularly about what she *didn't* know. So she poured the last of the coffee into her cup and went back out to the porch.

There were no boats visible from the green wicker chair—no charters, no freighters—though it would an exceptional day for being on the water, unseasonably warm and reasonably calm. And the coffee tasted better than the instant Karen had begun to buy since tea-drinking Jules had moved in. For convenience. Just one of several small accommodations she'd made for the sake of their relationship. As she thought about it now, her trip to the island to see about her father, to do her sister's bidding, had as much to do with Jules as with Susan. Jules came from a close family; she loved her parents "exponentially." More than once she'd encouraged an increase in Karen's communications with her father. Reconciliation.

Jules was right, in many ways. Karen had not been the most dutiful daughter for some time. Except for brief, perfunctory e-mails, she'd neglected her father, not to mention the other members of her family—Susan, their grandmother—even former friends. But was it Jules? Or was it something about Karen herself? Even *before* she and Jules had moved in together, her life had assumed the plot of a soap opera, Jules being simply the most recent in a series of intense and all-consuming affairs that had focused Karen's time and driven her affiliations for a number of . . . *years*, years during which her concentrations and commitments were like different stopovers on some grand world tour. Each new country was more fascinating and exciting than the last; and each became her favorite, for the moment—at the expense of any fondness for the country she'd just left.

Jules had been introduced to Karen by Lea, at a gay rally in Lansing. Lea and Karen were co-workers, answering the phones for PDI. At first, they'd shared lunch breaks—grousing about how unprepared some salespersons were when orders were called in. Only by way of a stray admittance had they discovered similar interests in intimacy. But their relationship outside of work was tenuous, at best. Personality differences they both recognized. Fortunately, it was nothing that affected their friendship at work.

Before Lea, Karen had been living with Max—Maxine—who had been one of the circle of friends Dan and she had hung out with during the years they taught at Jefferson Middle School. Before Karen moved in with Maxine, she'd been engaged to Dan, and for seven years she'd played future housewife to his future husband, one consequence of their having spent every moment of high school together, straight and faithful high school sweethearts—homecomings and proms, the Key Club and the choir—so certain of their future union that, after graduation, they'd registered for the same classes at the local college. All during high school, and then for seven years after, Dan had been the

only love Karen had known. A love that always felt a little defi-
cient to her, a little less than satisfying . . .

Max helped alter those perceptions, at first offering freedom
and change, *demanding* change, in ways that Karen thought were
liberating and exciting, though not always understood. For the
longest time she believed it was the *lack* of knowledge that defined love as she knew it. She fell in love with Max, a friend of
both hers and Dan's. Then Lea, when it was clear that Karen and
Max could never unloose their relationship from the memories of
Dan's friendship and prior claims to Karen's affections. And now
Jules.

Love. So why hasn't she returned the calls, knowing how
anxious Jules would be? Why was Karen instead sipping a cup
of coffee in her father's green wicker chair, and finding a certain
contentment listening to the exhalation of waves along shore,
the occasional screech of a gull? Why was this solitude—which
as a girl she'd complained was so boring and awful—suddenly so
soothing?

And why wasn't she more concerned—as Susan was—about
their missing father?

Because it was not the first time, for one thing. He had a history
of isolation and silence, at least with respect to his daughters.
While he never actually voiced disapproval of what they did or
didn't do, he often seemed to harbor disappointment in them,
like a gray fringe of clouds at the edge of a blue sky. He'd shut
himself off from them, communicate in merely obligatory ways.
Their mother had simply excused his behavior as "writer's blues."
He'd been known to retire into voicelessness for any number of
reasons—reasons that had nothing to do with his daughters—
and he was not in the habit of providing explanations, other than
those he hinted at in his columns and reviews, which he would
occasionally photocopy and send to Karen. (To be sure she'd
read them?) Certainly there was some intent in the one he'd sent

since her angry phone call after the birthday party—a review of a short story collection in which the same characters appeared throughout. "A book of stories," he'd written, "that could easily be read as an autobiographical novel. For sometimes it's not the details one puts in that gives a story unity; it's the details that one leaves out."

Like the details, perhaps, of the First Lady story, which Karen had been thinking about earlier, as the ferry *Emerald Isle* rumbled its way from Charlevoix to St. James. She'd fallen into a dreamy half-sleep on the ferry, dulled by the lake's unnatural calm—its surface barely broken by swirls of wave, like crescents of missed polish on a pewter serving tray—and lulled by the hum of the ferry's diesel engines. In her dream-state, the story of her father's affair with the governor's wife warped into a surreal timelessness. The girl in the dream was not young Marly, the caramel-eyed co-ed skinny-dipping in some limestone-rimmed, creek-fed pool in the Appalachian foothills, as Karen normally pictured her, an image based on surreptitious peeks at her father's college yearbooks from that time; rather, she was the prim, blue-dressed, pearl-necklaced woman who appeared so often in newspaper photos or on TV newscasts, just behind or to the right of the governor. Karen pictured her the way she is now, the way she knew her father would like people to picture her—for the joke, the incongruity—and yet, oddly, she imagined *him* the way he appeared in the photos from thirty-some years before—the wild curls, the long, bushy sideburns, and the cocky smirk he'd often touted. Marlene was in her fifties, proper, even bourgeois, the image of propriety and responsibility—a string of pearls, for god's sake; Dad was twenty, youthful and carefree, rough in his unseemly handsomeness and callous in his disregard for other people's feelings. In the dream, such an affair was more than simply a funny story. It was grotesque and scandalous, rife with disaster and tragedy.

Contentment, Karen decided, is an island somewhere off the coast of familiar. She found it ironic that one of the cottage's more compelling attractions was that the place did not foster in her any fond memories. Dan had been the only lover who'd ever taken the ferry out there with her, years before, during a time in their relationship when an island cottage held certain romantic notions. But he'd groused the whole time, their intimacy tainted by his sullenness. She couldn't recall exactly why. Still, nothing about the here and now was haunted by Dan's ghost.

Which was not to say he wasn't missed, at times. His confidence, the way he knew when to embrace and when to just stay near. At times, she longed for his cheap soapy smell, his hooded sweatshirts, even his laughter (which she'd more often thought sounded like the rasp of a small dog pulling at a short leash). But there is a lot she didn't miss, couldn't miss—his jealous tantrums and sense of control, the assumptions he'd made about her, about them, assumptions that eventually led to the breakup. In truth, Karen missed the friend she had, his generosity and kindness; but she didn't miss how stifled his friendship made her feel at times. She missed his self-confidence and assurance when she faltered; she didn't like his assumption that she was *always* faltering. She'd been smothered under his certainties.

Jules, fortunately, had many of Dan's good qualities. She was confident and assertive, a comfort in times of need. And yet. The aspects of Jules's personality that had recently begun to irritate Karen tended to be those same qualities that she'd eventually found irritating in Dan. Her confidence was—there's no better word—*stifling.* Even now Jules was waiting anxiously for Karen's return call, ready to give advice and to take action on Karen's behalf. She was prepared to charter a flight in a moment's notice, if asked. Jules wanted to be involved in *everything* that was going on with Karen, even the things Karen didn't care to share.

The twang of a rusty door spring rousted her from the wicker chair, where she'd fallen asleep. She found her father standing beside the refrigerator, a white plastic grocery sack dangling from his left hand. He looked pleased to see her, if a half-smile could be interpreted as *pleased*. But he didn't look surprised. *Of course not*, thought Karen. He'd have anticipated the visit. Susan would surely have left him a phone message or e-mail to that effect, a minor threat. It's even likely that he'd have gone to the store and bought enough groceries for their dinner.

He looked good, otherwise—a little thin, maybe, but healthful and rested. His face retained a bit of a late summer tan, though there was a slight yellowishness at the corner of his mouth, on either side of his gray-streaked mustache. And he was wearing what Susan called his "unfashionable fashion": faded jeans, an open flannel shirt over an off-white tee, a faded green baseball cap. It wasn't until he'd set the grocery sack on the counter and come to her for a hug that she noticed the gauze pad taped to his neck.

Still, he didn't say a word.

"We were worried," she said. He cocked his head and raised his eyebrows, as if he were questioning the concept. Karen read his mind. If he'd been in a talking mood, he'd have said *Susan was worried*. "Okay," Karen corrected herself, "*Susan* was worried."

"No need," he whispered. And winced. He reached for the half-sheets of used printer paper that he kept beside the phone, selected a blue Paper Mate from the assortment of pencils, pens, markers, and gewgaws that crammed a lopsided ceramic vase on the counter—Karen recognized it as the one she'd made in junior high—and wrote *I'm okay*, spelling out the word *okay*. It was like him not to abbreviate even the most common colloquialisms.

"Then why . . ."

He pointed to the bandage on his neck. *A small operation,* he wrote. *Temporary laryngitis.*

"What *kind* of operation?" she questioned. She hadn't intended the pitch of her voice to rise. "You had an operation and you didn't tell us?"

He pointed to the Post-it note beside the sink: WHAT'S THE POINT?

I'm fine, he wrote on the pad, and turned it for her to read. Then underneath he wrote: *It was benign.* He showed her again. The third time he wrote: *(heh, heh).*

Karen had caught the rhyme, his way of making a joke. She was not amused. "Cancer," she said flatly. "You had cancer and you didn't see a need to tell us?"

It was more like a cyst, he wrote. *What could you have done?*

"One of us could have been there, in case something went wrong."

Had something gone wrong, you would have heard.

She paused. He was right; there was nothing that she or Susan could have done. (Not that either of them would have made an effort anyway.) How could she be angry with him? She should be grateful that he didn't cause them undue worry, relieved that Susan's panic had been unfounded. Truth be told, the elder sister's anxiety was likely the reason why he'd chosen not to tell in the first place. Enduring Susan's well-meaning but meddlesome concern would have been worse than enduring radiation treatments alone.

Dear Karen, he wrote below his little poem, *How are you? I am fine.*

He'd once told her the story about learning to write pen pal letters in fourth grade. His teacher had informed the class *never* to begin with "How are you? I am fine." In an early act of defiance, he'd pledged to do so at every opportunity. All the letters Karen received from him, at Girl Scout camp or at college, began the same way: *Dear Karen, How are you? I am fine.* It was another one of his small jokes.

Curiously, his e-mails—mostly short and businesslike—seldom started like that.

"Surely you could still send e-mails, even if you can't talk," she said, "and Susan said that Robert McGurney was worried."

His eyebrows furrowed. *Bob knew,* he wrote. Then: *SUSAN!*

So she'd fibbed about his editor's lack of information in order to manipulate Karen into making the trip. Karen pursed her lips and shook her head: "That little . . ."

Her father smiled. *Dinner?* he wrote.

The fresh whitefish fillets he'd brought from town were a treat. As Jules didn't care for seafood, Karen had stopped preparing fish at home; she ordered it only when they'd go out. She concocted a side dish out of what she could find in the freezer and cupboard—peas and rice. For dessert, they split an ice cream cake that Karen's father had been saving, he wrote, *For a special occasion.*

At first, Karen answered his questions aloud. But by the time they'd gotten to the freezer cake, they'd both resorted to writing—his answers in blue ink, hers in black.

He described his operation. Then he asked about Jules. He asked how things were going. She wrote: *Everything's going OK. J is OK, sends her love.*

Her father raised his eyes to her—blue, tinged gray—and cocked his head theatrically, the way a mime would show disbelief. *Really,* Karen wrote. *Things are fine. There's nothing to tell.*

Good, he replied. *As it should be.*

Later, when they seemed to have come to a lapse of things to say, she wrote: *So, have you seen the governor's wife recently?*

He laughed and grabbed the bandage at his throat.

Karen dried as her father washed up the dishes; she felt four-teen again. Then they took a walk on the beach, where the breeze brought a hint of autumn off the lake, before settling into fa-miliar chairs on the porch. Karen called Susan and told her that everything was fine: that Dad had had a small tumor removed from his throat; that it was impossible for him to speak just now but that he'd been to a post-operation checkup today, as it was the day that the oncologist from Munson Medical Center kept his appointments in St. James, and that everything looked good; that he'd been at the doctor's when Karen arrived; that he'd not wanted them to worry . . .

"But he could have at least answered my e-mails," Susan said. "Ask him why he didn't answer my e-mails."

Karen looked at her father. "Susan wants to know why you didn't answer her e-mails," she said, loud enough so Susan would hear.

His shrug passed a kind of knowledge between them. Karen waited what she thought was an appropriate amount of time—time for him to write an answer, though he'd made no effort to do so—and then said into the phone: "There's apparently some-thing wrong with his Internet server. It's been infected by a virus or something. He's having trouble connecting."

He smiled and nodded.

Another ungainly silence filled the phone. Karen pictured her sister standing outside her house in Oakdale Farms, staring at the red bricks that defined the patio, her cordless phone cupped to her left ear, a cigarette in her right hand. Inside their smoke-free colonial, her husband Brian would be watching TV in the family room, their two daughters tucked properly in their beds upstairs, under matching Hello Kitty comforters.

She heard a sigh or a long release of smoky breath. "But he's okay," Susan said.

"*Yes*," Karen answered, definitively, as though Susan's state-ment had been a question.

"And he'll write when he gets back online?"

"She wants to know if you'll send her an e-mail *as soon as* you get back online," Karen said, emphasizing the emendation for Susan's sake.

Her father shrugged.

"Of course," she said into the phone.

What she doesn't know won't hurt her, Karen thought later, a consideration that was appropriate not only to a father's decision not to tell his daughters about a cancer operation—which he'd later confessed just happened to have been scheduled on their mother's birthday—but also to her fabrication of the truth concerning their father's neglect of e-mail. Wasn't it only fair to counter Susan's lie about his editor's worry with Karen's lie about his Internet service? *Tit for tat*, she thought. She didn't ask her father for the real reason, and he never offered an explanation.

Jules called twice during the time they walked after dinner and twice more as they sat on the porch and watched the last reflection of the sun fade on the lake's surface. But Karen had turned her phone off. She knew Jules would leave messages on voice mail, and she could imagine what they sounded like—the insistence, the concern. She decided they wouldn't talk again until she got back to their apartment, where she could explain, face-to-face, how the island was out of reach of her network and she'd not gotten the calls . . .

She slept on the porch, as she had when she was a young girl. She dreamt that she woke to the white warmth of sun on her face and was in the middle of a string of self-appointed curses at her oversleeping when she noticed her father standing at the porch door. He was wearing a bathing suit, a towel across his shoulders like a boa.

"What are you doing?" Karen said hoarsely, in a voice that

resembled what his voice had sounded like the night before, the few times he'd attempted to speak.

"Penguin swim," he said softly, and childhood summers came back to her in a splash: lake water screaming cold, goose bumps, the smells of alewives, Ivory soap, citrus shampoo.

It was a cottage ritual. When the girls were little, when their mother and father shared in the pleasures of parenthood and marriage, and when their summers were a series of weekends, a couple holiday weeks, and not what they would become later—the whole long season's worth of timelessness and irresponsibility and absence from friends—Karen's father would get up early, rouse whomever he could to join him, and take the first swim of the day—bathe actually, as though they were camping and did not have a warm shower just a few steps away. From Memorial Day to Labor Day at least—earlier and later in the season if they could stand it. He called it "the Penguin Club," and Karen had been its most faithful member.

"But it's *September,*" she said. "Labor Day is over."

"I was in recovery," he whispered. "I missed the last of the season."

"Isn't it too cold?"

He shrugged. She could see a plastic bottle of shampoo in one hand. The other gripped the ends of the beach towel together at his chest. He looked uncertain, possibly even a little scared. Like he didn't really want to go in, but he would anyway, out of nostalgia perhaps, or some sense of obligation. Or challenge. To prove something. Perhaps that he still could . . .

"Did the doctor say it was okay?" she asked.

"He didn't say I shouldn't," he whispered, and the look on his face made it obvious that it was a strain to form the words. "He said I could shower . . . just the same."

"It's *not* just the same," she said.

"Then you won't go?" he asked.

When Karen was younger, she had been sure she could tell

the difference between the pleading and mocking of his blue eyes. Now she was no longer sure. "The last of the season," he whispered.

It's a great story the way he tells it, Jules would say.

Yes, she answered. It would make a great story, if she crawled from the sleeping bag that she'd spread out on the chaise lounge, grabbed the beach towel that was folded on the green wicker chair, and raced her father to the water and the shock she would surely encounter there. And she'd be the only one who'd know how true the story was, whether she plunged in or not. Whether or not it was merely part of a dream.

It would make a great story, she repeated, a kind of explanation, perhaps, like the story of the time her father stopped talking, and of the events that transpired because of his silence—the events that changed forever the direction her life would take.

Acknowledgments

Grateful acknowledgement is made to the editors of the publications in which versions of these stories first appeared:

Boston Literary Review: "Within an Inch of the Burnished Knob"
The Driftwood Review: "A Real Deal"
Our Working Lives: "One Version of the Story"
Short Story: "The Good Life"

The author also wishes to extend his gratitude to:

The judges of the PEN Syndicated Fiction Award, for selecting "One Version of the Story," and Alan Cheuse for including its broadcast on National Public Radio as Program 79 of "The Sound of Writing."

The Sabbatical Leave Committee and the Board of Trustees of Ferris State University, for providing time away from the classroom, during which several of these stories were drafted or reworked.

And heartfelt thanks to:

The editorial board of the Made in Michigan Writers Series, for their faith in this book, and the good editors and production staff of Wayne State University Press, who so graciously worked it into its present form.

The friends and family that inform these tales.